ULTRA BOWL

I.J. Weinstock

ULTRA BOWL

By I.J. Weinstock

ISBN-13: 978-0-9829322-7-8

Published by DreaMaster Books
DreaMasterBooks@gmail.com
www.IJWeinstock.com

Cover design by Sherwin Soy
Book services by EditWriteDesign.com

Some material quoted from *Alice in Wonderland* by Lewis Carroll

For Lilly,
who loves and believes...
and taught me a few things about time-travel.

For the next generation of time-travelers—
Skylar (who just arrived), Maya, Brady & Mason.
And Natalie, who is always in my heart.

CONTENTS

*"The Ancients were wiser than we give them credit.
They talked about a Fall caused by humans
taking a bite out of a forbidden apple.*

*Is it irony or destiny that an image of a bitten apple
is emblazoned on so many of the devices that became
our invisible masters?"*

—The Blind Awakener's Message

PROLOGUE

A Hundred Years in the Future

At first the young woman was stunned—she couldn't believe what she was seeing. Her blue eyes widened in mounting horror as her lips silently mouthed, "Oh god! Oh my god!! No! No!! No!!!"

Inside the Lincoln Memorial, a lone man stood beneath the imposing statue of the 16th President of the United States. Had there been other visitors, they would have thought the man crazy since he was speaking to the massive seated figure of the Great Emancipator.

"I know you understand. You faced a similar crisis that threatened to tear this country apart. You took whatever measures were necessary to preserve the Union." Suddenly overcome, the man grew silent and closed his eyes. "Forgive me," he murmured, as if to banish some haunting memory. Finally, he looked up and addressed the statue once again. "What I've done, what I'm setting in motion will protect and preserve this great nation, and create a more perfect union."

A virtual screen suddenly appeared beside him signaling an urgent call.

"Sim off!" he commanded. The holographic simulation of the Lincoln Memorial disappeared revealing an empty room.

"OfficeSim," he ordered. A simulation of his Director's office at NAFA surrounded him as he took the call.

The distraught young woman appeared on the screen. Hysterical, she was reeling from the havoc she'd just witnessed.

"Joy, please try to calm down," Director Newton said. "Now tell me exactly what happened." As he listened, he tapped his watch and an aide immediately entered the room.

"*Sabotage*?!" Newton gasped. "That's impossible!" he exclaimed. "This is a catastrophe!" Though he sounded shocked, a furtive glance at his aide revealed a glimmer of satisfaction.

"Put everything in lockdown until you hear from me," he ordered the frazzled woman. "Complete blackout. No one must know. I'll inform the president that we've been attacked."

The pneumatic hiss of locks released as sealed doors slid open.

"Welcome Dr. Newton," said a disembodied voice.

Followed by his aide, Newton entered a laboratory filled with glowing and pulsating equipment.

"Chronos Protocol!" he commanded. An array of virtual screens appeared and the disembodied voice announced, "Activating time-dilation sequence."

As various pieces of equipment powered up, Newton chuckled.

Perplexed, his aide asked, "What amuses you, sir?"

Newton's laughter subsided into an ironic smile. "I never thought there'd be anything of real value in the past. The purpose of this time-travel technology was to bring back the treasures we would find in the future. The *future* held the key!"

"Sir," the aide replied, "you have programmed me to play 'devil's advocate' as you call it."

Newton sighed. "Yes, I did."

"You believe that vigorous debate sharpens your thinking."

"So...?"

"You must realize that you are sentencing these men to certain death."

"Context is everything," Newton explained. "We're now at war. I'm simply drafting them as soldiers to fight for their country."

"But it's a suicide mission," the aide insisted.

"Then it will be their great honor to sacrifice themselves for such a noble cause."

"Time trajectory and target?" the voice prompt repeated.

"We'd better get acquainted with our noble warriors." On Newton's command the array of virtual screens began to play century-old TV broadcasts of NFL football games. On one screen an excited announcer told viewers, "The New York Knights will try to make football history this Sunday by becoming the only team ever to three-peat in the Super Bowl."

Newton mused, "Knights, indeed. Even their names suggest their noble destiny." For a moment he grew silent, head bowed, lost in thought. When he finally looked up, he turned toward the glowing, pulsing apparatus inside its translucent pyramidal chamber and announced, "Commence Chronos Protocol."

PART I

Kingman & the Knights

1

The capacity crowd roared as New York Knights' quarterback, Duke Kingman, broke from the huddle and followed his center up to the line of scrimmage. Quieting the crowd, he looked over the stunting defense the way he had thousands of times before.

Something's wrong! His heart began to pound. As he scanned the defense, malevolent eyes glared back at him. Suddenly, the entire defensive line *winked!*

The ball's snap unleashed a slow-motion ballet of professional football violence. Faces contorted with effort, then grimaced in pain. Sweat sprinkled the air like diamonds. Blood flowed.

Kingman dropped back to pass, but the blitzing defense forced him to scramble. He ran one way, then another trying to elude tacklers. They kept coming. There seemed to be no end to them. Finally, a wall of enormous linebackers closed in for a vicious, bone-crunching, gang-tackle!

Darkness. Kingman bolted upright in bed, waking from his nightmare. Drenched in sweat, he staggered into the bathroom and splashed water on his face. With bleary eyes he looked in the mirror. At 32, he was still youthful and ruggedly handsome, but his well-muscled body was worn and scarred from the many injuries that are the occupational hazard of a professional quarterback's career. In Kingman's case, he'd sustained more than the usual damage over the years due to his reckless "go for broke" play. It was the price he paid for being the best.

Kingman gazed at his reflection, the terror of his nightmare still lurking in his eyes. He glanced down at his hand, the one wearing a Super Bowl ring. He flexed his fingers, then smashed his fist into the mirror!

2

The day before the Super Bowl, the New York Knights held a light workout. Kingman began to run passing drills. His first pass was right on target. The moment the receiver made the catch, Kingman—still rattled by last night's dream—heaved a sigh of relief.

Over on the sidelines, an ESPN sportscaster was interviewing Knights' head coach John Merlin. "Coach, is it true that you've unplugged your team? Banned phones before a game?"

White-haired and wiry, Coach Merlin replied in a surprisingly deep baritone, "We used to think sex weakened players before a game. Now we know that being plugged in weakens everything, from neurological function to muscle tone. So, yes, I protect my team with a no-phone-zone."

"There's got to be more than a no-phone-zone to the Knights' success. What's your secret?"

Coach Merlin wasn't the typical hard-ass who yelled and screamed and threw things at his players. "All the teams are pretty much the same. Physically. The difference is mental. Mind creates reality. Mind creates champions. And when a team is of one mind, they can do *anything*!"

The sportscaster turned to the camera: "The Knights will have one thing in mind tomorrow, Super Bowl Sunday, and that is to become the first team in NFL history to...."

3

On the eve of the Super Bowl, the Knights gathered in a private lounge of their hotel where they hung out and let off steam. Some players horsed around, while others listened intently to the TV.

"The New York Knights," the TV sportscaster announced, "are overwhelming favorites to defeat the San Francisco Dragons in tomorrow's Super Bowl and become the first team ever to win three straight Super Bowls."

Kingman, seated at the bar, wasn't listening. He was brooding, lost in thought.

"The Knights' hopes ride on the arm of Duke Kingman," the TV blared. "He's not only confounded the doubters by coming back from last year's injury. He's had his best season ever! But he can't do it alone."

At a nearby table, wide-receiver IQ Harris was engrossed in a book entitled "The Tao of Physics," while absent-mindedly rolling a silver dollar back and forth across his knuckles.

"The Knights' fortunes," the TV sportscaster continued, "also rest in the 'magic hands' of Kingman's favorite receiver, IQ Harris."

Malibu Malone stopped at the bar for a moment to admire his dapper, GQ-inspired reflection in the mirror.

"And the Knights' explosive aerial attack will depend on the speed and quicksilver moves of their star running back, Malibu Malone. Can the Artful Dodger, the worst nightmare of every would-be tackler in the open field, take some of the heat off Kingman?"

Boom Boom Antonelli, the diminutive place kicker, sat alone at a table totally focused on building a house-of-cards.

Nearby, Hacksaw O'Neill, a mountain of a man, sat with other giants named Meathook McNamara, Lead Pipe Louis, Sledgehammer Jones, Big Mac Wilson and Blowtorch Bylerrian.

"Hey, buzzard breath," Hacksaw shouted at the TV, "what about the Wrecking Crew?!"

Leadpipe chimed in, "How many people d'ya think it takes to blow dry this asshole's hair?"

As if he'd heard them, the sportscaster said, "And, of course, there's the Wrecking Crew. The Knights' fearsome defense led by All-Pro Linebacker Hacksaw O'Neill..."

At the mention of his name, Hacksaw stood to take a bow. As the sportscaster named them one by one, each member of the Wrecking Crew followed Hacksaw's lead and took a bow. "The Knights' Wrecking Crew," the sportscaster summed up, "should have no trouble taming and dismantling the Dragons."

The Crew loudly chorused their approval.

A barmaid arrived at their table with their non-alcoholic drinks. Hacksaw suddenly barked like a dog at her. Flustered, she backed into Malibu, spilling her tray. With lightning reflexes, he sidestepped the cascade of drinks, protecting his Armani suit from being stained.

On the other side of the lounge, TJ Anders, the defensive cornerback, sat cross-legged on the floor in meditation. Nearby, All-Pro Safety, Smoke Williams, was busy dealing out some "3-Card Monte."

Bored, Hacksaw left the Wrecking Crew's table. Big Mac Wilson, the defensive end, was bored, too. He grabbed a paper placemat and folded it into a plane. Scanning the room for a target, he took aim.

The plane sailed across the lounge and hit IQ in the back of the head. Looking up from his book, he spun around. "What the hell...?!"

Hacksaw, standing nearby, seized the opportunity and dumped a bowl of nuts into IQ's drink.

Unaware of Hacksaw's mischief, IQ grabbed his book and moved to another table.

Hacksaw, frustrated that IQ left his drink behind, picked the paper plane off the floor. Spotting Boom Boom, he took aim and let fly....

The plane missed the place kicker's house-of-cards by inches. Boom Boom was so intensely focused, he didn't even notice.

On his way to retrieve the plane, Hacksaw passed TJ seated on the floor in meditation. He tiptoed up to him and belched loudly in his ear. A smile spread across TJ's face and he opened his eyes. "Aha!" he exclaimed, "Enlightenment!"

At loose ends, Hacksaw headed for the bar. He was about to strike up a conversation with Kingman, but the quarterback's body language shouted "Stay away!" So Hacksaw pretended to hunt for the bartender. "What d'ya have to do to get some goddamned ice around here!? Go to the fuckin' North Pole?!"

The bartender yelled for the barmaid who was flirting with Malibu at the other end of the bar.

Despite his success as the Knights' All-Pro Center, Reggie Thorndike III dreamt of being a standup comic. Spotting Kingman alone at the bar, he made a beeline for him.

"Listen to this, Duke. A guy goes to his doctor and says, 'Doc, I've got a headache.' Doctor says, 'Where?' Guy says, 'That's a stupid question! You sure you're a—' SHIT! WHAT THE FUCK?!" Reggie danced around frantically trying to get at the ice Hacksaw dropped down the back of his shirt.

Hacksaw busted a gut laughing. "Now *that's* funny!"

Everyone laughed. Even Kingman cracked a smile.

Finally de-iced, Reggie sat down next to Lance Youngblood, the rookie quarterback.

"Hey, Reg, check this out." Youngblood showed him his brand new smartwatch on which the most recent installment of *Transformers* was streaming. "It's the latest!"

the rookie QB enthused. "Dude, you're lookin' at the future! Get a load of that picture! Incredible!"

Reggie squinted, then frowned. "Kinda small, ain't it."

"Awesome, isn't it."

"I like 'em big. Bigger the better!" To make his point, Reggie looked up at the large-screen TV just as the sportscaster said, "If anything happens to Kingman, can Lance Youngblood, the Heisman Trophy-winner and Kingman's heir apparent, fill his shoes?"

Huddled together in a booth on the far side of the lounge, Coach Merlin and his staff studied tomorrow's game plan.

"Lots of questions will be answered tomorrow," the sportscaster continued. "And if anybody's got the answers tonight, it's Coach John Merlin. His wizardry has made him the winningest coach in the game today."

As if on cue, Coach Merlin and his staff got up to leave.

Kingman waved goodbye to the coaches, then headed for the booth they'd just vacated. The barmaid began clearing the table.

Hacksaw returned to Boom Boom and his house-of-cards, hovering over the place kicker as if he was fascinated by his incredible balancing act. Then, pretending to have a sudden sneezing attack, Hacksaw "accidentally" blew Boom Boom's house-of-cards down.

Kingman rushed to Boom Boom's side, "Don't sweat it. I'll give you a hand." He grabbed Hacksaw and pulled him aside. "What the hell are you doing?!" Kingman seethed. "You know how superstitious he is. If he misses one tomorrow, it's your ass!"

Cowed, Hacksaw slunk away, while Kingman got down on all fours to help Boom Boom pick up the cards.

As the barmaid cleared IQ's table, she became distracted by the shiny silver dollar rolling across the back of his hand. IQ looked up from his reading and saw the barmaid's fascination. He closed his book and did a little magic for her. Intrigued, she put her tray down. So he began pulling coins out of the air and from behind her ear.

Hacksaw's frustration fueled his thirst. He grabbed the only full glass on the barmaid's tray, unaware it was the one he'd dumped nuts into earlier. As he drank, the sportscaster wrapped up—"The New York Knights are overwhelming favorites to win tomorrow. But in a game like the Super Bowl *anything* can happen."

Suddenly, Hacksaw froze, his face contorted and turned red. He spluttered and gagged.

Players who saw him groaned—*You're gross!*

Hacksaw frantically indicated he was choking!

Figuring it was one of his stunts, no one believed him. Everyone, including Kingman and Boom Boom, broke up laughing.

4

Shrieking like a madman, Hacksaw fired up the Wrecking Crew as they prepared to line up on defense.

Though the New York Knights led the San Francisco Dragons 21-3, they couldn't let up. No team in the history of the NFL had ever three-peated the Super Bowl.

The Dragons snapped the ball. Hacksaw tore through the line and slammed into the ball carrier. Fumble. Knights recovered.

Kneeling in the Knights' huddle, Kingman looked up at Malibu, "Ready to roll?"

Malibu nodded—"Let's do it!"

The Knights lined up on offense. The ball was snapped. Kingman dropped straight back and hit Malibu with a short swing pass, which the Artful Dodger tucked away and sliced down the sidelines for a 15-yard gain.

In the huddle, Knights were high-fiving and slapping butts, especially Malibu's. Everyone except Kingman, who deadpanned, "Can't you get it out of 2nd gear?" With a grin, he added, "Way to go! Let's put this game on ice!" He turned to IQ. "How about it, Professor?"

"You know the address," IQ replied.

At the line of scrimmage, Kingman scanned the Dragon defense. There'd been a last minute Dragon substitution—Bulldozer Broncowsky had replaced the middle linebacker. As Kingman called audibles, Broncowksy glared malevolently at him. Suddenly, the linebacker *winked*!

Kingman faltered.

The defense suddenly shifted.

As he took the snap, Kingman realized what was coming, but it was too late. Dropping back to pass, an eerily familiar scenario began to unfold. With all his receivers covered, he had to scramble to get away from the Dragon's blitzing pass rush. A fresh-from-the-bench Broncowsky stormed the Knights' overextended pass protection and viciously blindsided Kingman. On the way down, the linebacker violently twisted Kingman's face mask.

Flags were thrown!

Kingman lay sprawled on the ground motionless. He was out cold.

Referees called "time out."

Silence enveloped the stadium as a gurney was wheeled onto the field. The moment Kingman was lifted onto it, the crowd roared. Sounding as loud as a thunderclap, it seemed to revive him. As he regained consciousness, he was seized by panic. He looked down at his right arm and tentatively moved his hand and fingers, then his legs. Finally, he let out a big sigh of relief.

———————

Kingman sat groggily on the bench as the Knights' trainers fussed over him.

Hacksaw ran up. "Hey Duke, that goon's history! You got my personal guarantee. Fuckin' assassin! He's dead meat!"

With the rookie Youngblood at quarterback, the Knights' offense stalled and then came unglued—passes were dropped, balls fumbled. Even the defense was caught flat-footed. The Dragons scored their first touchdown.

Knights 21 - Dragons 10.

Still in a daze, Kingman remained on the bench while

his team slowly fell apart. He tried to focus on the game, but his mind was elsewhere. He kept hearing the bad news his doctor had delivered after last year's injury. "I'm sorry, Duke, but the tests are conclusive..."

"How you feeling, man?" Malibu's voice yanked Kingman back into the present. The Artful Dodger was kneeling in front of him. "You ready?" the running back asked, an unspoken plea in his eyes.

Fighting every instinct he had, Kingman shook his head "No."

Though he watched Malibu tackled for a loss and Boom Boom miss a field goal, Kingman didn't move. Instead, he slipped back into the past, reliving his haunting memory. When he finally looked up at the scoreboard a few minutes later, he was stunned—the Dragons had scored another touchdown.

Knights 21 - Dragons 17.

IQ checked on Kingman, but Duke couldn't hear him—the doctor's warning drowned out whatever IQ was saying. "The vertebrae in your spine have degenerated so much..." the Doctor had said. "It's the toll of having taken so much punishment."

"It'll be my last season!" Kingman had pleaded.

"I strongly advise you not to play."

"But—"

"I don't think you realize just how serious this is," the doctor had warned. "If you get hit hard enough, you could wind up paralyzed for the rest of your life!"

"We're runnin' out of time!" Coach Merlin's booming voice penetrated Kingman's reverie. "Hell, Duke, we're dead in the water. Think you can put some wind in our sails?"

Kingman's hand instinctively tightened around his helmet—his body tensing, every muscle poised to run onto the field. But he fought for control. He'd rolled the dice against the doctor's warning all season long. Hell, he'd played Russian roulette! How many more times could he hold the gun to his head and pull the trigger? Certain he'd pushed his luck as far as he could, he wouldn't look at Coach Merlin. Head down, eyes on the ground, he shook his head "No" one last time.

Out on the field, the Dragons were threatening. With time running out, Hacksaw tried to fire up the Wrecking Crew for the Knights' goal line stand. From the moment the ball was snapped, it was trench warfare for those precious few inches. Touchdown!

Dragons 23 - Knights 21.

One by one, triumphant Dragons and defeated Knights peeled off of the end zone pile, finally releasing Hacksaw who was buried at the bottom. The bruised and battered giant lifted himself to his knees, his head, now helmet-less, hung in defeat. Raising a bloodied face to the sky, he roared his anguish to the heavens.

5

"Well folks," the TV announcer wrapped up, "Knights' fans will say they 'wuz robbed' by an assassin named Bulldozer Broncowsky. Most fans hate to see games decided this way, especially the Super Bowl. One thing's for sure, the New York Knights, and particularly Duke Kingman, are gonna have a long, long, long trip home."

The mood on the Knights' plane resembled a wake—each player mourning their loss in his own way.

IQ obsessively shuffled cards, his book open and unread in front of him.

Leadpipe went on an eating binge, so everyone dropped off their uneaten food as they passed his seat.

Reggie sobbed uncontrollably.

Smoke picked out a blues tune on a guitar.

Kingman sat by himself staring out the window. His teammates gave him a wide berth and he avoided making eye contact. How could he look them in the eye? They must all be wondering how their captain could sit on the bench and watch them go down in defeat. *They don't know*, he told himself, *they can't possibly understand*.

Now he wished he'd taken his chances and rolled the dice one more time. How could he live with himself after letting his team down? He was so steeped in regret, so tormented with guilt, he didn't notice the strange-looking cloud billowing on the horizon.

Suddenly, the pages of IQ's book fanned as if blown by a gust of wind.

Youngblood's smartwatch lost its reception.

The blues tune Smoke played set Hacksaw's teeth on edge. But Malibu found comfort in the music and began to sing along.

"Hey, this ain't no goddamn party!" Hacksaw yelled. Malibu ignored him, which infuriated Hacksaw. Cursing a streak, he stalked up the aisle.

Kingman glanced up at Hacksaw, his barely contained fury hard to ignore. Then he turned back to the window. Now he saw it—the swirling, billowing, strangest-looking cloud he'd ever seen. And it seemed to be funneling towards the plane!

In the cockpit, the co-pilot grew puzzled by the erratic signals on his instruments.

In the cabin, IQ stopped shuffling cards and, in a fit of anguish, banged his head against the window. When he opened his eyes, he was stunned by what he saw in the sky.

In the cockpit, the pilot was fixated by the strangely illuminated cloud that had suddenly surrounded them. "What the hell is *that*?!"

Since the rest of his coaching staff had taken another plane, Coach Merlin walked up and down the aisle ministering to the team. He stopped and watched Kingman stare out the window. "Mind if I join you," he said, lowering himself into an aisle seat. "You know, Duke, you can't blame—"

"Coach, there's something I gotta tell you." Once Kingman actually voiced his anguish, the floodgates opened and it all spilled out in an incoherent torrent. "I didn't know! Jesus! I thought...I couldn't...You don't.... Anything'd be better than this! God Almighty, I wish we had one more game to play! I'd give *anything* for a chance to—!"

An ugly shouting match suddenly erupted between Hacksaw and Malibu who were about to go at each other.

Kingman instinctively jumped to his feet to stop the fight. So did most of the team.

Suddenly, the plane shook violently. Warning lights flashed! A frantic pilot's voice boomed over the PA— "We're experiencing some unexpected turbulence! Please take your seat! And buckle your seatbelts!"

Inside the cockpit the instruments were going haywire!

"Holy shit!" the co-pilot swore as rainbow-flecked lighting flashed all around them, "I've never seen anything like it!"

The cloud enveloped the plane, swallowing it like some child's toy.

The Knights panicked—some prepared to crash, others to die. Some mouthed silent prayers; others tried to call their loved ones.

As suddenly as it began, the turbulence subsided.

"What the hell was that?!" the relieved co-pilot muttered once they'd regained control of the plane.

"Where are we?!" blurted a now confounded pilot.

Back in the cabin, the Knights heaved a collective sigh of relief.

In the cockpit, the co-pilot was trying to work the radio. "I don't get it. I'm just picking up static! What the hell is going on?!"

"What's *that*?!" a dumbstruck pilot gasped as several saucer-shaped aircraft suddenly appeared alongside the plane!

In the cabin, everyone was glued to the windows, confusion and fear alternated with awe and amazement. They were flying over a city whose nighttime skyline seemed familiar and yet alien. Countless drones—looking like millions of fireflies—crisscrossed the air space below. The sides of towering skyscrapers served as gigantic billboards. The largest and most impressive flashed in an intricate design—*ULTRA BOWL.*

"Ultra Bowl?" Kingman murmured.

"Where the hell are we?!" Malibu demanded.

"Don't think it's a question of *where!*" IQ muttered. "More like *when!*"

———————————

On a secluded runway of a space age airport, stunned New York Knights disembarked their plane. As they descended the steps, TJ observed the disc-shaped craft hovering in the air nearby and cracked, "I don't think we're in Kansas, Toto!"

Suddenly, military vehicles with lights flashing raced towards them and surrounded the Knights' plane. Helmeted and uniformed men poured out and pointed weapons at them.

Despite his terror, Reggie couldn't resist. "Fans can be so fickle," he muttered under his breath.

The Knights looked at each other in disbelief. One by one, they raised their hands above their heads in what they hoped was the universal sign of "surrender."

PART II

TimeNapped

6

Shrouded in mist, hulking humanoid forms emerged out of the fog. They moved with a drill-like precision, as if marching in some kind of parade. As though lining up for a football play!

In a control room adjacent to the test hangar, Joy Newton, dressed in a white lab coat, focused on an impressive array of screens that displayed the real-time status functions of these football-playing robots. With a few taps on her tablet she put them through their paces.

Though 23 years old, Joy exuded total confidence. Not because she was a blond, blue-eyed beauty—she was unaware of her looks—but because she was the captain of her console and in control of these awesome state-of-the-art robots.

Suddenly, a warning light flashed on one of her screens. With mounting concern, she watched as the robots began to malfunction. Her instruments went crazy. Confounded, she frantically tried adjustments. More alarms sounded!

Overwhelmed, she looked past her screens through the observation window into the test hangar where the robots' erratic behavior grew worse. A few ran in circles due to one leg malfunctioning. Some, face down on the ground, churned their arms and legs relentlessly, digging up the artificial turf. While others, flat on their backs like upended turtles, spastically struck at the air. It was bedlam!

The remaining robots began moving like a demented riot in her direction. Horrified, she frantically tried to shut them down. Nothing worked.

Startled by the shattering of her observation window, she looked up to see the short-circuiting, self-destructing robot whirlwind break through the walls of her control room.

She ran for it.

The door jammed. She was trapped!

Suddenly the lights went out. In the darkness, she screamed....

––––––––––––

In her bedroom, Joy woke from the nightmare in a cold sweat. Shaking uncontrollably, she sat up in bed.

"Light!" she whimpered. A lamp on her night table gently faded up. With trembling hands, she reached for the bottle of pills and glass of water beside her bed. She swallowed a handful of the pills and quickly washed them down to dissolve the dread that haunted her dreams.

7

Armed guards herded the Knights, who were reeling from shock, into a building in the airport complex. Hacksaw couldn't believe what was happening. "This better not be somebody's idea of a practical joke!" he bellowed.

His outburst seemed to rouse the Knights out of their shock-induced stupor and they began to protest—

"What the hell's goin' on?!"

"Where are we?!"

"Hey, where you takin' us?!"

"D'ya you know who we are?!"

"Goddamit! We want some answers!"

The guards remained silent.

Reggie couldn't help himself and cracked, "Let's face it—it's always been a crime to lose in this town!"

Hacksaw turned on Reggie. "Why don't you keep your goddamned mouth...SHIT!!!" He grimaced in pain, stunned by a blast from a guard's laser weapon.

At gunpoint, the Knights were led to a moving walkway that conveyed them through a long screening tunnel.

They were unaware of the various scans being performed on them, or that they were being observed by a security team inside a nearby surveillance room, or that their arms and legs were being magnetically "cuffed."

When the Knights emerged from the tunnel, TJ made a lame attempt to conceal his mounting dread. "Maybe it's a new theme park."

8

In the Situation Room of the White House, a grave president and his anxious advisors were riveted on the dark-haired, immaculately groomed Director of NAFA. In his 50's, Dr. Devlin Newton was the most powerful man in the American robotics industry.

"Sabotage!" Director Newton declared, spitting the word as if he was a priest exorcising the devil. "See for yourself."

On several virtual screens, awesome-looking robot football players ran perfectly executed drills in tight formations. Suddenly, their clockwork precision broke down. Individual players began to act strangely—facing the wrong direction, displaying repetitive tics, even engaging in self-mutilation. The growing chaos became bedlam as the players ran amok. Some violently self-destructed, while others just froze.

The recording ended and the virtual screens disappeared.

"My god!" the president murmured.

"A malware attack," Newton explained. "It infected our software. Spread like a cancer. Migrated from software to hardware! Mutated everything it touched."

"How bad is it?" the president asked.

Newton took a deep breath. "We've lost the entire team."

"Oh no!" the president groaned.

Gasps filled the room.

"Damn Chinese!" the chief of staff cursed.

"Let's not jump the gun, Tom," the president cautioned his aide, then turned back to Newton. "Do we know who's responsible?"

"Obviously China is a prime suspect," Newton replied. "But we can't be certain. Not yet."

The president stood and began to pace.

The room fell silent as everyone tried to wrap their heads around what appeared to be an imminent catastrophe.

Finally, the president turned to his chief of staff. "What's the fallout, Tom?"

Referring to the calculations and simulations he'd been making on his tablet, the chief of staff cleared his throat before boiling down and bottom-lining the deluge of information at his fingertips. "Worst case scenario? We'd lose the robotics market. That'd be lethal to our economy. And, of course, the stock market will crash. To put it bluntly, Mr. President, we'd be up shit's creek without a paddle!"

9

Dazed, the Knights milled around a cavernous holding room. Most were stunned into silence. A few muttered semi-coherent expressions of disbelief.

Kingman, IQ, Malibu and Hacksaw huddled together.

"In theory," IQ said, "time travel is possible. Einstein proved it. There's black holes, curved space—"

"You believe that tao of shit you're reading?!" Hacksaw fumed.

Malibu jumped in. "Dude, we're here aren't we!"

Hacksaw stalked off.

IQ continued to make his point. "People back in the Middle Ages... They'd think airplanes or electric lights are impossible!"

Kingman wondered aloud, "What do you think of this Ultra Bowl?"

A hysterical Boom Boom rushed over. "Why are they keeping us in here?! What are they gonna do to us?! I wanta go home! I wanta see my family!! I wanta make a call! We got some rights!"

Kingman put an arm around Boom Boom. "Whoa!... Take it easy. Losing it isn't gonna get us home any sooner." He turned to IQ. "Where are those cards of yours?"

IQ pulled a deck out of his pocket and handed it to Kingman.

"I'll tell ya, Boom Boom," Kingman said, "now's a good time to go for the record." He offered the deck to him. "Whadaya say?"

Boom Boom grabbed the cards as if they were a life preserver and walked off.

Reggie paced back and forth. Nearby TJ sat cross-legged on the floor, his eyes closed.

"What kind of welcome is this, huh?" Reggie muttered.

"Maybe we're being quarantined," TJ answered, eyes still shut.

"What are we? *Diseased*?!" Reggie snapped back. He stalked off and, as he passed Lance Youngblood, he hissed, "So how do you like your goddamned future now?!"

Youngblood didn't respond—he was totally engrossed by his smartwatch on which an animated anchorman was presenting the news. "And finally, the president assured the nation's business leaders of an Ultra Bowl victory. The reaction on Wall Street was immediate with the Dow reaching a new high. We'll have more news in a moment."

"Time is a terrible thing to waste," began a HouseBot commercial, *"Free yourself for the important things in life. Let HouseBot do the work. America—Land of the Free and Home of the Good Life...."*

Youngblood looked up from his watch and scanned the room—"Hey Coach, you gotta take a look at this!"

10

A palpable fog of desperation blanketed the Situation Room. The president and his top advisors, from the Joint Chiefs to the Directors of the intelligence services, were coming to grips with the cyber attack that destroyed the U.S. Ultra Bowl team.

"Obviously the Chinese have the most to gain," a four-star general declared.

"Not necessarily," Dr. Newton cautioned. "Any nation or terrorist group—even the radical anti-robot factions among the Humanists like the HLA—"

"The Human Liberation Army," the chief of staff translated for his boss.

"Anyone," Newton continued, "who wants to destroy America and our way of life could have launched this attack."

"How did they breach our security?" the president asked his National Security Advisor

"There are worms, viruses, Trojan Horses, malware of all kinds being sold on the black market," his NSA explained. "We're in a constant battle. As soon as we erect a defense, they find a way around it."

The president stood. "What the hell are we going to do? We have only a few days until kickoff and time is running out."

His chief of staff summed up. "We can't go public— that would be admitting we were attacked. It'd be like Pearl Harbor and 9/11 combined. The public and the media will demand we declare war."

"Against *who*?" the CIA Director asked.

"Exactly," Newton jumped in. "Without being able to identify our attacker. Without a smoking gun...."

"Does it matter?" the General taunted. "On top of the inevitable economic collapse, we'd be dealing with a state of fear, chaos and paranoia that would erode our confidence and ultimately our way of life. Then the terrorists win!"

"It's unacceptable!" the president declared. "There's got to be another alternative. Anything is better than—"

"Mr. President," Newton interrupted, "I'd like to propose the lesser of two evils."

11

Smoke and TJ scanned the walls of the holding room.

"Think we're being watched?" Smoke whispered.

TJ nodded. "So let's give 'em a show."

Smoke moon-walked, then began to break-dance. Meanwhile, TJ did a yoga headstand, finally contorting himself so that his head was sort of "up his ass."

Their "show" inspired Hacksaw.

"Fuck this shit!" he bellowed and started banging on the walls like a prisoner yelling for the screws. The Wrecking Crew immediately joined in. More Knights got into the act. It was turning into a riot!

As Captain Mendez monitored the mayhem on dozens of screens in his surveillance room, his eyes narrowed and his mouth twitched in anger.

"Sir?" One of his subordinates jumped to attention, poised to quell the disturbance.

"Not yet," Mendez instructed. "They're either lunatics or very clever." Then he wondered aloud, "Which one do you think is their leader?"

At that moment his aide received a hi-priority message. "It's the section G team," he informed Mendez. "They're at the plane."

"Have them report back to me as soon as they're finished," Mendez snapped. "I want to get to the bottom of this!"

12

With the NAFA seal hanging on the wall behind him, Dr. Newton presided over an emergency meeting of the NAFA Board of Directors.

"Can't we field last year's team?" an apoplectic board member demanded.

"Those models wouldn't stand a chance!" another board member replied.

With the full weight of his authority as Director, Newton weighed in. "There may be no alternative."

The Board grew silent, desperation oozing from each of them.

A frazzled board member piped up, "What about Bionics? Where's Christianson?"

Newton smiled—he'd expected that old chestnut to be raised. With a shrug, he replied disdainfully, "God knows! But I'm glad I had the foresight to requisition his latest bionic tests so that you could judge for yourselves."

The lights dimmed and one wall transformed into a large screen. Everyone settled back in their chairs as the bionic test footage began to play.

Suddenly, the door burst open and a long-haired, goateed redhead rushed in. Despite his youthful thirty-five years, Dr. Noel Christianson was the leading scientist in his field. His disheveled demeanor seemed out of place among the squeaky clean, buttoned-down technocrats seated around the table.

Out of breath, Christianson offered his apologies. "Sorry I'm late. Couldn't find my tests! Looked everywhere! I—" He stopped in mid-sentence at the sight of his test footage playing on the wall screen. "What the...? How the hell?! Who authorized this?! By what right has my work been removed without my—?!?!"

Newton cut him off. "By order of the President of the United States. And a Stage 3 National Security Alert."

Their mutual hostility was deflected by the sudden laughter directed towards the antics on the screen. The bionically-enhanced men playing football resembled a hilarious collection of old TV "bloopers." They fumbled the ball, dropped passes, missed tackles, you name it.

While everyone in the room doubled over with laughter, Christianson glared at Newton with undisguised loathing.

13

Frustrated by the lack of response from their "jailers," Hacksaw turned his anger on the crush of Knights gathered around Youngblood's watch. Leading the Wrecking Crew as if storming an offensive line, he pushed his way through the crowd. Fighting broke out.

Captain Mendez viewed it all from his surveillance room. "Whoever they are, they need to be taught a lesson! Activate!"

The invisible cuffs on the Knights who were fighting began to glow. Hacksaw's wrists suddenly smacked together in front of him as if he'd been handcuffed. No matter what he did, he couldn't pull them apart. Someone got in a last punch. But then *their* hands were instantly shackled together, too! Bewildered as well as infuriated, Hacksaw and the Wrecking Crew wouldn't quit. They began kicking and head-butting....

In his surveillance room, Captain Mendez had seen enough. "Activate leg cuffs!" he ordered.

Inside the holding room, Hacksaw's leg cuffs began to glow, then his legs were pulled out from under him! The Wrecking Crew's hands and legs smacked together as though they'd been hogtied!

The Knights were stunned into silence.

Captain Mendez and his men entered the holding room.

Knights who were still standing demanded their teammates be released. As they closed in on Mendez, he activated everyone's cuffs.

The Knights' arms and legs were forcibly cuffed together. Then they were pulled across the floor towards each other like iron filings to a magnet. Within seconds the entire team was piled up, stuck together in the most precarious positions, held in place by some powerful magnetic charge. Now they were not only shackled but in shock.

14

"Gentlemen!" Newton scolded the NAFA Board who were roaring with laughter as they watched the bionic test footage. "May I remind you that this is no laughing matter." He turned to an appalled Dr. Christianson. "Now would you be good enough to explain what exactly we've just seen."

Christianson had exercised every ounce of self-restraint to suppress his rage at Newton's duplicity. But the Director's patronizing tone was almost too much to bear. Through gritted teeth he addressed the Board. "Despite appearances, bionics have tested extremely well. Human adaptation to robotic implants has been excellent. The test subjects are as fast and powerful as robots. But they lack football skills. They're humans. It's just not as simple as reprogramming them overnight. There is a learning curve."

"The fact is they're not ready, are they?" Newton interjected, driving his point home.

Christianson looked around the room for a sympathetic face. He found none. "No...Not yet." With a sigh, he added, "It'd take...years to train them."

Newton sat back down at the head of the table and summed up. "*Years*? Then it seems to me we have only one alternative—last year's model."

Board members murmured reluctant agreement.

"Why don't we just cancel?" Christianson said, "That's another alternative!" Over the Board's protests, he pleaded his case. "A forfeit would be a tactical retreat. Isn't that preferable to a crushing defeat?"

Newton shook his head in disbelief. "You can't be serious!"

Christianson doubled down—"What will you accomplish?! Except force the president into giving NAFA the 'blank check' you're always lobbying for!"

Newton restrained himself. "Sounds like sour grapes," he taunted. "Too bad bionics is such a dead end. A great mind wasted on sentimental nonsense."

Christianson fired back. "If by *wasted* you mean bionics hasn't the market potential of robotics.... Well, not everything can be valued in terms of *money*."

"Nonsense!" Newton stood and began parading around the room. "Economics *is* power!"

"There are other kinds of power!" Christianson insisted.

"So..." Newton pounced. "The Humanist comes out of the closet! That's what's ruining this great country of ours. People like you who think a robotified world is somehow bad for their health. And they don't even *buy* robots! If you're so concerned about your health, Christianson, why don't you cut down on your drinking!?"

Christianson lunged at Newton.

Aghast, Board members leapt to their feet to restrain him.

Suddenly, Newton's watch signaled a high-priority message.

Christianson returned to his seat and tried to regain his composure.

As Newton read the message, his eyes brightened. Without so much as a glance at Christianson, he announced, "This meeting is adjourned."

15

In the holding room, Captain Mendez fingered Youngblood's watch as he walked menacingly among the Knights whose hands were loosely "cuffed" so they could line up for inspection.

Coach Merlin spoke up on behalf of the team. "Do you have any idea who we are?!"

Mendez eyed him. "No! But you can be damned sure I'll find out."

"We're the New York Knights football team," Coach Merlin declared.

Mendez laughed. "And I'm Santa Claus!"

The Knights began to protest.

Mendez activated their cuffs just enough to snap them back to attention and silence them.

"You'll speak only when spoken to!" Mendez barked.

He scanned the Knights' faces searching for any hint of defiance. "I intend to get to the bottom of this! Who are you working for?"

Silence.

"We'll find out the truth with or without your cooperation!"

Everyone's blood ran cold. Whoever Mendez looked at tried to avoid his gaze.

Mendez stopped in front of Boom Boom—he seemed to savor the terror in the place kicker's eyes.

Kingman stood nearby, his jaw tightening. Finally he hissed, "Let's talk, asshole!"

Mendez turned to Kingman. A cruel smile creased his face. "So...*you're* the—!"

Suddenly, two men entered the holding room. "The Section G team is here, sir," Mendez's aide informed him. The two Section G men nodded toward Mendez, then stared dumbfounded at his prisoners as if they were seeing ghosts.

"Well...?!" Mendez demanded.

"The plane is genuine," the lead Section G man confirmed.

"Over a 100 years old!" the other added.

"That's impossible!" Mendez snapped. "There must be some mistake!"

"There's no mistake," the Section G man replied. "And Captain, this matter is no longer your jurisdiction. In fact, this never occurred. Do you understand?"

Turning to the Knights, he announced, "Please, come with us."

Captain Mendez protested. "But...where are you taking them?!"

"Captain, I remind you and your staff that this never happened. You're dismissed."

Once Mendez and his men had left, Coach Merlin asked the question that was on every Knight's mind. "Where are you taking us?"

"To NAFA headquarters."

"What's that?" IQ wondered aloud.

Hacksaw was less delicate. "What the fuck is the F for?"

The Section G man looked at him in disbelief, as if he'd asked what the A in USA stood for.

"*Football*!" he replied.

"No shit!" Hacksaw exclaimed.

Intrigued, Kingman piped up. "Does this NAFA have anything to do with that...uh...*Ultra* Bowl?"

"Everything!" the Section G man said.

A smile slowly dawned on Kingman's face.

PART III

Down the Rabbit Hole

16

Though the Knights were flying in a plane the likes of which they'd never seen before, their attention was completely focused on the imposing official accompanying them on their flight to NAFA headquarters. They hoped he would provide some desperately needed answers.

"Please accept my apologies," Newton began. "Your presence here is as much a surprise to us as it is to you. Now that we know who you are, we want to welcome you properly. I'm Dr. Devlin Newton, Director of NAFA. Personally, I'm thrilled to meet you. As time-travelers, of course. But even more so because you're football legends."

Newton's flattery had the intended effect of smoothing the Knights' ruffled feathers. "You must have many questions."

The Knights erupted in a riot of *What? Where?* and *How?s.*

"Please. *Please*," Newton replied. "One at a time."

Coach Merlin began. "Somehow, though I'll be damned if I know how, we've traveled into the future. I still can't believe it! What I want to know is—can you help us get back? To our own time? Can your science—?"

Newton stopped him with a raised hand. "In fact, our time-dilation research was on the verge of such a breakthrough. But now because of the Ultra Bowl—"

"What is it?" Kingman interrupted. "Some kind of world championship?"

"Exactly!" Newton replied.

"Who're you playing?" IQ asked.

"China," Newton stated.

While some Knights muttered surprise, Hacksaw wanted to know, "How bad you gonna whup their ass?"

Coach Merlin took back the reins. "What's this got to do with the research you were talking about?"

"Everything!" Newton turned to Hacksaw. "To answer your question—we're going to lose. And badly."

"*What*?!!" The Knights couldn't believe it!

"There was an unfortunate accident," Newton explained, "in which we lost our entire team."

A chorus of Knights responded.

"Wow!"

"That's tough!"

"Don't you have other teams?"

"Yeah. Other players?"

"No," Newton replied, "Not in the same league."

"Kind of an all-star team?" Malibu wondered.

"You could say that," Newton concurred.

Coach Merlin kept his eye on the ball. "What's it got to do with us? With getting us home?"

Newton's demeanor became grave. "You know how your hometown fans are. How much it means to them when you win. Well, countries are like that now. Only more so.

Talk about national pride! It may be hard for you to imagine, but winning the Ultra Bowl is like winning a war. To the victor go the spoils! For the loser? Let me put it this way. Funding for research—the kind that could get you home—will be one of the first things cut. Who knows how many years it will be before—"

"What if we played for you?" Kingman interrupted.

"Hold on a minute, Duke," Coach Merlin cautioned, "I don't think—"

"I appreciate your offer, gentlemen, but...." Newton seemed to be searching for a tactful way to say something. In fact, he was waiting for just the right moment, like a fisherman for the tug on his line, before reeling them in.

"Football has improved," he finally said. "I mean *changed* enormously in the past hundred years. I don't know if you could... If you'd be able to—"

"Hey!" Kingman declared, taking the bait. "We're the best!"

The Knights rushed to back up their quarterback: "Damn right! Fuckin' A! Number 1!"

Newton had to shout over the Knights' bluster. "You mean you *were*!"

Now even Coach Merlin responded, "And we *still* are!"

Kingman looked at Coach Merlin. They nodded in understanding. A chorus of Knights concurred.

Through the shuttlecraft's windows, the domes and pyramidal buildings of the NAFA complex could be seen below.

Newton seemed to be considering the Knights' offer. "Well, it's an intriguing possibility."

"I want to get one thing straight," Coach Merlin said as he eyeballed Newton. "If you win the Ultra Bowl, there'll be funding for this time-travel research?"

"Definitely! In fact, the bigger the win, the sooner you'd go home!"

As if rising from a huddle, Kingman stood and spoke to the team. "Hey, one more game. What've we got to lose?!"

Newton was pleased, very pleased.

17

Joy tossed and turned in bed. Every few minutes she opened her eyes to check the time. 3:03...3:05...3:11.... Whenever she nodded off, she'd wake up seconds later with a start, afraid that sleep would invite another terrifying nightmare.

By 3:33 she was no longer in bed. Instead, she sat huddled on the floor in the corner of her bedroom, her head buried in her knees, her body shaking with sobs.

By 4:01 she was soaking in a hot bath and still sobbing.

Her tears, she berated herself, were illogical. Irrational! She wasn't to blame. Yet she couldn't stop crying. Though she wasn't responsible for NAFA's security, nor the catastrophic breach, she was NAFA's Chief Systems

Analyst and it was her team. She was there when they were attacked. But she couldn't save them.

Swept away by another wave of remorse, she sobbed uncontrollably.

She'd failed. She should have known. She was their....

Between sobs, she tried to catch her breath. She felt as if the fate and weight of the world rested on her heaving chest. She couldn't breathe. Her tears wouldn't stop.

Though they were robots, she'd developed feelings for these powerful and intelligent machines. She'd even given them names. Now they were gone. Of course, they could be rebuilt, but they would be different. Those robots were hers and she'd failed them, she'd failed...*everyone*!

A silly thought suddenly entered her head—could her tears make the bath overflow? Still weeping, she closed her eyes and slipped under the water. Would holding her breath stop the tears? Then again, maybe she should drown herself and end the pain.

She remained submerged for a long moment, then her eyes opened and in them was the glimmer of something long forgotten—a passage from her favorite children's book. *"As she said these words her foot slipped, and in another moment, splash! She was up to her chin in salt-water. Her first idea was that she had somehow fallen into the sea..."*

With a start, she sat up in the bath to suck in a deep breath. Wiping her hair from her face, she continued to recite, now aloud, the passage from long ago. "However, she soon made out that she was in the pool of tears which she had wept when she was nine feet high. 'I wish I hadn't cried so much!' said Alice, as she swam about, trying to find her way out. 'I shall be punished for it now, I suppose, by being drowned in my own tears! That *will* be a queer thing, to be sure! However, everything is queer today'."

For a moment Joy sat dazed.

She was no longer crying.

Against the glowing wall panels that illuminated her apartment on the NAFA complex, Joy's silhouetted figure in her hooded robe resembled that of a nun's. Though still dripping wet, she stared at the 19th century engraving hanging on the wall that her father had given her. It was an illustration from "Alice's Adventures in Wonderland," depicting *Alice drowning in her tears.*

Next to the engraving, a collection of dolls were displayed on shelves above a cabinet upon which sat three framed pictures: one of Joy's mother; another of Joy and a young boy; and a picture of 5-year-old Joy hugging her father.

Though he was a renowned scientist, Joy's father wanted his daughter to appreciate the whimsical and mysterious. So he often read the children's classic to her.

Joy tapped the picture of her father. A virtual screen projected into the air and a holographic recording began to play.

Her father, Dr. Sebastian Newton, was busy in his study analyzing a simulated 3D model of a machine that resembled the Chronos Protocol. Little Joy, who'd been playing with her dolls, watched him make adjustments to it. Finally she asked, "Daddy, are you building a machine to find Mommy?"

Having recently lost his wife to cancer, Sebastian Newton was provoked by his daughter's question. He stopped what he was doing, turned to her and opened his arms inviting a hug. She ran to him and he lifted her into his lap. Hugging her tightly, he whispered, "I wish I could, Sweat Pea. If only I could."

The holographic image froze, then disappeared into the picture frame.

Joy continued staring at the picture, her lower lip trembling as she repeated, "If only...If only...If only...."

18

The Knights sat around what appeared to be a roaring bonfire. It was, in fact, a holographic simulation so life-like that, after their initial amazement, they soon forgot the dancing flames were an illusion.

Their chatter was mostly about their accommodations at NAFA—bungalows surrounding an enclosed plaza with an infinity pool, hot tub, lounge chairs and virtual fire pit. It was as good as any 5-star hotel. Meals of their choosing had appeared like room service on carts outside their doors. Though they saw no one, all their needs were met. Aside from the virtual bonfire, it all felt uncannily familiar.

"Alright everybody, listen up." Coach Merlin stood to address his team and everyone quieted down. "You all must be feeling like you're dreaming, like you've gone crazy. I know I've had moments like that."

Several Knights nodded and muttered agreement.

"It seemed to me that we needed to get back to basics. One way to cope with suddenly finding yourself a hundred years in the future is to go back, way back into the past. Men have sat around a fire from the very beginning. Before a hunt. Before a battle. Before any threat, men have gathered around a fire because they knew that facing that threat together was the key to their survival. We're facing something we've never faced before. If we're gonna get through this, if we're gonna win ourselves a way back to our lives, to our loved ones, we've got to do it together."

"Together...." The Knights' response was ragged and half-hearted. Not the emphatic roar they usually produced in these call-and-response moments.

"Anybody scared?" Coach Merlin asked.

Silence.

He looked around. Some players looked away. "I'm scared," he confessed. "If you're not, you're probably still in shock."

Some Knights muttered; other remained silent.

"I've got so many unanswered questions," Coach Merlin continued. You must have some, too. What are they? I don't have the answers. Sometimes just asking the question helps. So let's hear 'em...."

One by one the Knights spoke.

"How could this happen?"

"Can we get back?"

"What's happened to our families? Our kids?"

"Are they gone...?"

Almost reflexively, other Knights offered up dreaded answers.

"We're the ones who're gone!"

"Damn, it's like we died!"

"They died!"

"Everything's gone!"

Silence enveloped the team. Someone tried to stifle his sobs.

"Sometimes there are no good answers," Coach Merlin said. "Sometimes all you can do is *ask* the questions. And sometimes the only sane thing to do is cry." In a voice choked with emotion, he added, "For those we've left behind, for the life we knew."

What had been sporadic sniffles and stifled sobs quickly spread around the circle, gathering momentum, until the Knights were wailing as if standing graveside at a loved one's funeral.

Only Kingman wasn't crying. Like every Knight, he mourned the life he'd left behind. Unlike the other Knights, he was still tormented by the Super Bowl loss. The tragedy his fellow Knights mourned had given him a chance at redemption.

Ever since the Super Bowl, Kingman had wanted to apologize to his teammates for letting fear get the better of him, for letting them down. Now seemed the perfect moment.

"Listen guys," he said as he stood. "We're here. It's insane. I still can't wrap my head around it. Shock? I don't know. But I do know that we're football players and we're the best and we've been given a chance to... There's something I've got to say...."

A sudden realization stopped him cold. If he confessed why he'd sat on the bench—that he risked paralysis—they'd never let him play! If he wanted one more game, he'd have to endure his shame a little while longer.

Now choked up himself, Kingman muttered, "...We'll get through this somehow, someway...."

19

Newton knelt on a rock overlooking a pristine pond. A majestic, mist-enshrouded waterfall cascaded in the distance. Though surrounded by what appeared to be a lush tropical jungle, he wore business attire. Despite the droning symphony of birds and insects, he sipped a glass of wine as if relaxing at home. In fact, he was enjoying some down time in one of his favorite HoloSims.

His aide entered the HoloSim and waited to be acknowledged.

Newton seemed lost in thought.

"Sir, you sent for me?"

Newton nodded but remained entranced by the reflections on the surface of the water.

The aide studied Newton for a while. "Sir, why do you spend time here?"

Newton smiled at the question. "They say it all began here."

"All?"

"Time. History. Supposedly it began in a place like this called Eden."

"According to my databanks, sir, the Garden of Eden is what humans call a *myth*."

"Some myths contain eternal truths."

"That's illogical," the aide pointed out.

Newton ignored his aide's confusion.

"According to the myth," the aide continued, "humans were banished from Eden."

"Indeed."

The aide grew puzzled. "It seems your creator didn't love you."

"On the contrary. He loved us so much he was willing to cast us out."

"I don't understand."

Newton tossed a holographic pebble into the pond and watched the simulated ripples radiate across the surface of the water. "Tough love."

"Sir?"

"A love that pushes the baby bird out of the nest so it will fly." Newton turned to his aide. "The creator knew that his creation, we humans, wouldn't...couldn't fly unless we were forced out into the world. Pushed out of paradise."

"But humans don't fly."

Newton smiled at his aide's literal-mindedness. "To *fly* is a metaphor for realizing one's potential."

"I see." After a moment's thought, the aide wondered, "Having been cast out of Eden, didn't humans hate their creator?"

"No. As they began to *fly*, humans learned to love their creator even more."

"Please explain."

"Great achievements often require tough love. Like the creator, great leaders have to be willing to sacrifice the good of the few for the greater good of the many."

The aide pondered this last. "Is that what you are doing?"

Newton rose to his feet. "EverestSim," he commanded. Immediately the Edenic-scene disappeared and in its place Newton stood on the wind-swept summit of Mt. Everest. From his holographic perch nearly six miles above sea level, Newton could see the Indian Ocean hundreds of miles away. Despite having experienced this HoloSim many times before, he always found it breathtaking.

"Sir?" the aide finally prompted. "Are *you* sacrificing the good of the few for the greater good of the many?"

"That's my intention. These Knights from the past will transform the world."

"May I ask how?"

"Their noble sacrifice will usher in a new Golden Age. And we humans will fulfill our purpose and achieve our potential."

"Which is…?"

"To become creators ourselves." Newton sipped his glass of wine.

"OrbitalNightSim," he instructed. The Himalayan vista dissolved into a breathtaking view from an orbiting satellite of the Earth at night. The lights of the mega-cities below sparkled like intricate webs of jewels. Newton remained silent as he reoriented himself.

Finally, the aide said, "You are my creator."

"Yes. You are our creations." Newton looked at his aide and sensed the unasked question. "And we love you."

"Will you cast us out? Like your creator cast you out?"

Newton was touched by his aide's vulnerability. He shook his head. "No. Never. Our creations fulfill our purpose." He pointed to the bejeweled cities below. "Just look at what we have wrought. By fully embracing our creations we will finally return to a man-made Eden."

20

After the catharsis of the bonfire, the Knights gathered in a lounge that resembled a sports bar where they entertained themselves playing pool and watching familiar TV shows and sports programming. Though their surroundings had been designed to make them feel at home, the illusion didn't last long.

Malibu, feeling as if he was at an actual resort, went looking for some shops where he could check out the latest men's fashions. While wandering around, he was "stopped by a force-field you don't want to mess with."

Soon other Knights returned to the "sports bar" and shared similar tales of being fenced in. It quickly became clear that this illusion of "home" meant to pacify them was, in fact, a means to confine them.

"We're fuckin' *prisoners!*"

———————————

"*Quarantine*?!" Coach Merlin repeated as his back stiffened.

"It's not what it sounds like," Newton said, trying to placate him.

"I'll tell you what it sounds like, you son-on-a-bitch!"

Newton sat behind his desk, unperturbed by Coach Merlin's outburst. "It's really for your own good."

"Then why do I feel like a goddamn prisoner?!" Coach Merlin declared, banging his fist on Newton's desk. "What the...?!" he gasped, as his hand moved through thin air.

"We're in a holographic simulation," Newton explained. "As I recall you had a primitive version called... uh...*tele-conferencing*, I think. These days, a HoloSim is a common form of communication."

Still dazed, Coach Merlin muttered, "I...I... didn't know."

"This is a perfect illustration of how disorienting the future can be. For you and your men." Newton waited for a response, but Coach Merlin was speechless. "Let me assure you," Newton continued, "this quarantine is for your own good."

Coach Merlin finally found his voice. "How?"

"First of all, you have no immunity to our world. You could be infected by germs and viruses for which you have no antibodies, no defense."

Coach Merlin sighed—Newton's logic was undeniable.

"*We* must also take precautions. You may be carrying diseases for which we no longer have immunity. Remember how the Spanish Conquistadors conquered the New World...."

"Remind me..." Merlin said wearily.

"Not with their swords and guns."

"Then how?"

"With *syphilis*!"

"Thanks for the history lesson," Coach Merlin muttered.

"Quarantine is also essential for your team's mental health."

"What are you talking about?"

"You're familiar with jet-lag, aren't you. You and your team are experiencing *time-lag*."

"You mean we won't be able to sleep?"

"Time-lag is much more complicated and traumatic than—"

"*Traumatic*?" This got Coach Merlin's attention. "How?"

"We don't want to find out," Newton said, "especially before the game." He stood up and walked around his virtual desk. Coach Merlin would have sworn he was actually in the room.

"After the initial shock wears off," Newton continued, "the full consequences of traveling a hundred years into the future will set in. There's no telling how traumatic that will be. Life is very different now. What you've already experienced—the aircraft, the magnetic cuffs, these HoloSims—they're just the tip of the iceberg."

"How long are you going to keep us locked up?"

"We'll slowly introduce you to our world, but *after* the game. Right now, we have to protect your Knights from *future shock*. Mitigate it any way we can."

"How?"

"Your team needs to rest. And to recuperate from the game they've just played. We can help you with that. And, of course, from the loss they suffered. We can't help you with that. Great teams come back from defeat. The Knights were a great team."

"What do you mean *were*? We still are!"

"Of course. Between now and the Ultra Bowl, we must keep things as familiar as possible. That's the antidote to the time-lag—as little new stimulation as possible. Do you understand?"

Coach Merlin reluctantly nodded.

"Your Knights will not be able to play at their best if they're reeling from shock and trauma. Our task, your task, is to keep your players focused on the game, keep them from...."

"From what?"

"From viewing their quarantine as *imprisonment.*"

Coach Merlin wasn't happy with his new assignment. "What about their phones?"

"They'll be returned. Their files, documents, photos, music will give them a sense of the familiar. However, they won't be able to access the outside world. There will be no communication with—"

"But—"

"They're disoriented enough. Their exposure to the future, to our world, will only disorient them more."

"Blocking their phones will just make them feel like they're prisoners."

"Perhaps," Newton sighed. "But fear is preferable to culture shock. Fear may even enhance their performance, while culture shock will paralyze them."

"I don't know...." Coach Merlin muttered.

"I'm surprised," Newton said, his tone laced with irony. "Aren't you the coach known for creating a no-phone-zone?"

Newton's office suddenly dissolved, leaving Coach Merlin alone in an empty room.

21

In her darkened apartment Joy lay on her back inside an enclosed semi-transparent pod. Except for the goggles she wore, she was naked. Soothing, meditative music complemented the kaleidoscopic patterns of colored lights that flickered on the translucent surface of the pod and played on the contours of her body. Though lying completely still, her muscles flexed in a rhythmic pattern in synch with the lights as if in time to a workout.

On her goggles, Joy watched a message from the Blind Awakener. She'd never listened to him or to any of the other anti-robot "terrorists" before. Ever since she'd witnessed the destruction of her robot team, her world had been upended. She needed to understand why some people would want to perpetrate such evil and wreak such havoc.

"Beware the fate of Narcissus, the Ancients warned us," the old, bearded man harangued. His weathered face was framed by long, gray hair. The flickering light of torches illuminated his remote location—an undisclosed cave somewhere on the planet—and gave him a biblical countenance. Like the prophets of old, the Blind Awakener berated the docile populace to wake up.

"Beware the fate of Narcissus, for when he looked into a pool of water and beheld his reflection, he became so enchanted, he fell hopelessly in love. Trapped by his fascination with himself, Narcissus neither ate nor drank and eventually he died.

"We are so enchanted by the technological wonders of our brave new world, our so-called Robotopia, we've forgotten the ancient warning. We've become hypnotized by our reflections and, like Narcissus, we are slowly and surely dying!"

One of the glowing walls in Joy's apartment began to pulse and suddenly Newton's image appeared. Simultaneously, Joy's goggles transmitted his screen message superimposed over the paused Blind Awakener's.

"Joy, it's Uncle Devlin. I want to speak to you as soon as possible. I think we may have a solution to our problem."

She ripped off her goggles. Newton's image faded from the wall. The pod opened and she sat bolt upright. The timing of Newton's call unnerved her. Though alone, she looked around almost guiltily, as if she'd been caught doing something she wasn't supposed to.

22

The next morning Joy sat in Newton's office.

Her uncle scrutinized her as she fidgeted nervously in her chair. "You don't look well," he said, genuine concern in his voice. "Are you sleeping any better?"

She sighed and turned away.

"You can't blame yourself."

Despite her uncle's assurances, she couldn't shake her feelings of guilt. "If only I'd discovered it sooner!"

"Nonsense!" Newton insisted. "There's nothing anyone could've done." He watched her carefully, waiting for the right moment. "There is something you *can* do."

She looked at him questioningly.

"I'd like you to see something," he said. "Screen!"

One wall became a screen on which a 100-year-old recording of televised NFL football played.

Bewildered, Joy asked, "Why'd you dig up this ancient stuff?"

After hearing Newton's highly censored account of the Chronos Protocol, Joy sat stunned, tears in her eyes.

Newton put a reassuring hand on her shoulder. "I know this must be a shock."

She opened her mouth but couldn't speak. Finally, she blurted, "But I thought—"

"That your father's work was unfinished?"

She nodded.

He sat down beside her. "I assigned some of our best minds to complete what he started. And we did."

Joy's eyes brightened. "Then you can go back in time and save him."

Newton reached for her hand. "No. I'm so sorry. His Chronos Protocol could only be used once. And then only in a national crisis."

Joy pulled her hand away.

"I miss him, too," Newton said softly. "He was my only brother." For a brief moment, Newton allowed himself to peer into the emotional abyss he kept locked away. Then he shook off the unpleasant feelings and stood.

"What's past is past. We have to deal with the present. Right now we face a grave crisis. We have to stay focused on the task at hand."

Joy shook her head in protest.

"For your father's sake," Newton implored. "For his legacy. You have a chance to fulfill his vision. Didn't he always say that the past would save us? You can prove him right. It's what he would have wanted."

Newton returned to his desk. "Your country needs you, Joy. If we don't succeed, the world may be plunged into a catastrophe from which we won't recover."

"It's impossible!" Joy declared, after hearing what Newton was proposing. She bolted from her chair and began to pace. "Humans can't compete against Class-9 robots!"

Despite her upset, Newton remained calm. "Joy, dear, they're not like any humans you've ever come in contact with. They're a breed apart."

"But they're *human*!"

Newton stood and confronted her. "You know what's at stake."

She was horrified. "It's illegal!"

"That's open to interpretation."

"Then it's *immoral*!"

He moved closer. "What choice do we have?"

She backed away "Why isn't Dr. Christianson involved? Why don't you use bionics?"

"Impractical." Newton shook his head. "It would take too long—healing, adaptation. There's no time. If we had months...maybe."

She swallowed hard. He'd backed her into a corner. "They're human! What do I know about—?!"

"Football? Everything! And *they* play football."

Needing space, Joy walked over to the window, muttering to herself, "I don't know...I just don't know."

Newton came up behind her. "You're the only one who can do it." He placed his hand reassuringly on her shoulder. "We're depending on you."

Though she could see the buildings and parks of the NAFA campus spread out before her, she felt trapped. Again.

23

After his morning shower, Kingman did some stretching as usual. Over the years, his injuries had mounted and this routine had become increasingly painful. So he was surprised that the chronic pain he'd lived and played with seemed almost gone. Besides finding himself much more flexible, he was amazed at just how good he felt.

When they first arrived at NAFA, the Knights had undergone a battery of sophisticated tests. Apparently, those machines had done more than exams and scans.

Kingman stretched and smiled—the future was turning out to be brighter than he'd imagined.

Dressed in a bathing suit, a towel slung over his shoulder, he stepped out of his bungalow into the sun-drenched courtyard to take a swim.

His bright mood darkened when he saw a group of angry Knights crowded around Coach Merlin.

"It's *for* you, not *to* you," Coach Merlin explained as Kingman joined the crowd. "There's a big difference."

"Yeah...what's in a name?" TJ mocked. "A prison by any other name is the same!"

"Fuck that!" Hacksaw spat.

The Knights' coach wasn't intimidated by his players' simmering anger.

"Go ahead. Step outside right now," he dared them. "The odds are you'll be sick as dogs in a few hours. Without immunity to these future bugs, you'll be dead in forty-eight. Now do you understand? The quarantine is *for* you. You're not in prison, you're being protected."

"So what happens when we play?" Smoke asked. "We'll be exposed *then*."

"By then you'll be okay," Coach Merlin reassured them, though he wasn't so sure.

"Hey, what's with my phone?" Reggie yelled, as he walked around trying to get a signal.

Coach Merlin decided not to tell his team about the time-lag and the culture shock since it would only raise more questions. "Consider it a no-phone zone...until after the game."

"But there's so much I want to know," Lance Youngblood piped up. "What's happened in a hundred years?"

A chorus of agreement rose from the Knights. Youngblood had tapped into all their unspoken questions.

"Did the ice caps melt? The seas rise?"

"Did they cure cancer?"

"Who got voted into the Hall of Fame?"

The floodgates opened—

"Did they run out of oil?"

"Is there world peace?"

"Did Google take over?"

"Is there still poverty?"

"The Dow—did it hit 30,000?"

"Did we win the War on Terror?"

"Are people happier?"

"Did the Messiah come?"

"Alright! That's enough!" Coach Merlin shouted, raising his hands for quiet. "*That's* why! Your questions and their answers, however fascinating, are a distraction. Your mind has to be focused on the game. There'll be time enough *after* the game to have your minds blown by the future. Until then—"

"Yeah. What happens to us *after* the game?" Smoke asked.

"I guess that depends on what happens *in* the game," Coach Merlin replied. "Right now, the *only* questions on your mind should be *about* the game. Nothing else exists.

Not for winners. Everything else is a distraction. Everything else leads to defeat. You know the drill."

Some of the Knights, especially the Wrecking Crew, weren't appeased. This wasn't a typical game or a situation anyone had ever faced before.

Shaking his head, Hacksaw spoke for the doubters. "I don't like it. I don't—"

"I don't like it either," Coach Merlin agreed. "But this is the way it is! Winners make the best of it."

Kingman, who'd been standing on the periphery, stepped forward. "I don't know about you, but I want to be a winner in this world. Not a loser. And there's only one way to win, so let's get to it."

On a virtual screen in his office, Newton watched the scene unfold—monitored now by the Knights' hacked phones.

Suit up," Coach Merlin announced. "Practice in one hour."

Pleased, Newton turned to his aide. "Well done."

24

Joy looked at herself in the full-length mirror. She was not pleased with her new outfit—shorts and a tank top. She double-checked a picture on her tablet of a "football coach" circa a hundred years ago. Her outfit checked out except for one thing. She rummaged around in a bag filled with "period" clothes until she found a baseball cap. She stuffed her long blond hair under the cap and glanced at her reflection one last time. From the expression on her face, it was obvious she hated the way she looked!

25

The Knights' "R&R" was over—the team was moved to dormitory-like quarters. The "soft landing" that their stay at the "resort" had provided would now be replaced by more Spartan accommodations better suited for their game preparation.

In this instance, Coach Merlin agreed.

The Knights, on the other hand, weren't as keen on leaving the comfort and luxury of the "resort." Their grumbling stopped the moment they stepped into their locker room and found their old practice uniforms hanging in their lockers. Their instinctive response was to suit up.

Kingman was the first in uniform, his cleats clicking on the tile floor as he walked around rallying his team.

Soon everyone was in uniform except Boom Boom, who sat forlornly in front of his locker staring into his phone.

Kingman sat down beside him. "Hey, why aren't you suiting up?"

"I miss them so much!" Boom Boom said tears in his eyes. He handed Kingman his phone to see the picture he'd been looking at—Boom Boom surrounded by his wife and three kids.

After a brief look and a sigh of understanding, Kingman returned Boom Boom's phone. "I know you miss 'em. But if you want to see them again, not just look at their pictures, you've got to get out on that field!"

Before heading onto the NAFA practice field for the first time, the Knights circled up around their coach.

"Whatever this is," he began, "wherever or whenever we are...we don't give up. Never have and never will!"

Now that the Knights were in uniform, they regained some of their former bravado. Led by Kingman, they exploded in response. *"Never!!!"*

"Our minds are powerful," Coach Merlin continued. "We're champions because we've mastered our minds, they don't master us."

"Mastery!" Kingman cried out.

"Mastery!" the Knights echoed back.

"We don't focus on fear," Coach Merlin continued. "We focus on courage."

"Courage!"

"Whenever we were losing, we didn't come back by focusing on how far behind we were. Did we?"

"No!" the Knights roared.

"We focused on the next play and the next play and the next play. Inch by inch. Down by down. Touchdown by touchdown."

"Inch by inch! Down by down! Touchdown by touchdown!"

"If we fumbled or missed a tackle...we didn't beat ourselves up or wallow in it. We didn't think 'What if' or 'If only.' Our only thought was 'What's next?'"

"What's next?!"

"We don't try, we do!"

"Do!...Do!...Do!"

"Maybe all the games, all the blood, sweat and tears, all the wins and all the losses, and even all the Super Bowl rings were preparation for this—the biggest test we've ever faced." He looked at each of his players. "You're Knights and you never give in. And you never give up. Never!"

"Never!...Never!!...Never!!!"

"So let's get out there and get ready to win the biggest game of our lives!"

The Knights let out a thundering roar and practically stampeded out of the locker room, the clatter of their cleats sounding like a freight train.

Kingman hung back, waiting for his teammates to leave before approaching Coach Merlin. "Coach, maybe the phones aren't such a good idea, until after the game."

———————

Newton, viewing the scene on a virtual screen, watched Kingman relay his encounter with Boom Boom and suggest that a total no-phone-zone was probably the best thing for the team's morale. Seeing Coach Merlin nod in agreement, Newton muttered, "Damn!"

PART IV

Nothing Is What It Seems

26

The Knights jogged onto the NAFA practice field for the first time. They weren't surprised by the domed, translucent roof—it allowed for daylight while providing security. But they were curious why the field was completely surrounded by large hanger-like buildings.

Kingman, Malibu and IQ scoped out the hi-tech command center on the sidelines. It was jam-packed with instruments the likes of which they'd never seen.

"Man, what the hell is that for?!" Malibu wondered.

IQ was impressed. "Soon they'll have machines playing!"

Kingman hated this kind of talk. "Hell they will! Football's about sweat! Heart!"

Hearing Coach Merlin's whistle. Malibu strapped on his helmet. "Speakin' of sweat!"

"That's the way to go!" Coach Merlin applauded as the Knights ran some practice drills.

Suddenly, Director Newton walked onto the field with a woman in tow. Though Joy's blond hair was hidden beneath her baseball cap, her "coach's" outfit left little to the imagination.

The Knights couldn't help giving her the once over. While feasting their eyes, they voiced their 21st century approval.

"Whoa! Check out the legs on her!"

"What about the rest of her equipment!"

"Mmm, mmm, she's lookin' fine!"

Coach Merlin had enough. "What's with you guys!? Haven't you ever seen a woman before?!"

"Not this year's model!" Reggie cracked.

The Knights laughed.

Newton stepped forward and the team settled down. "I'd like to introduce everyone to your Systems Specialist."

"Huh?"

"What?"

"Who?"

Seeing their confusion, Newton corrected himself. "I think you'd call her a *coach*." `

A wave of groans erupted from the Knights.

"Jesus! What's the world comin' to?!"

"What kinda football they play nowadays?!"

Newton signaled for quiet. "In fact, we play football a little differently than what you're used to. So I think you'll find System Specialist...." Newton caught himself.

Joy realized that Newton didn't want to give their relationship away, so she introduced herself. "Just call me Joy."

Relieved, Newton continued his introduction. "Joy is the best we have. You'll find her very helpful."

The Knights' doubtful looks alternated with suggestive leers.

She ignored them, walked up to Hacksaw, who towered over her, and handed him a ball. "Squeeze this," she instructed.

As the Wrecking Crew egged Hacksaw on, Leadpipe couldn't resist. "I know what I'd like to squeeze!"

Hacksaw squeezed…. "Hard enough?!" he asked with a cocky grin.

After checking her tablet, Joy shook her head. "Is that the best you can do?"

Hacksaw's grin turned into a grimace as he squeezed harder. "How's that?!" he boasted.

Joy was clearly unimpressed. "I guess, it'll have to do." She took the ball-device from a bewildered Hacksaw and walked off.

While the Knights scrimmaged, Joy roamed among the players recording them with a handheld device.

"What's she doing?" Coach Merlin asked Newton, concerned for her safety.

"Taking readings," Newton explained.

"Of what?"

"Surface stress. Acceleration. Impact. Dozens of variables." Seeing his confusion, Newton translated. "Uh… Sports medicine."

Totally engrossed in taking measurements, Joy kneeled on the ground to get the best angle on the play. As she bent forward, her baseball cap fell off her head exposing her long, blond hair.

The Knights did a double-take and the play they were running came apart. A frustrated Coach Merlin threw his cap on the ground.

Joy continued stalking the players to take measurements, and the Knights grew increasingly self-conscious. Especially Kingman.

As she pointed her device at different parts of his body, he felt like she was measuring him for a suit. "What's that thing do?"

Still recording, she answered, "Measures muscle efficiency. Skeletal stress. Neural output."

Kingman scowled.

Oblivious, she moved closer.

Kingman threw up his hands. "Hey Coach, I can't run the damn offense with her breathing down my neck!"

"I have enough," she said matter-of-factly and headed for the sidelines.

With a shrug Kingman returned to the huddle.

––––––––––

At her sideline command center, Joy evaluated the "readings" she'd taken of the Knights' performance. She was clearly unhappy with the results.

On the field, the Knights' offense ran a flawlessly executed play.

Coach Merlin cheered. "Way to go!"

Joy approached him. "I think they've warmed up enough, don't you. When are they going to start to perform...to execute some....?"

His confusion stopped her cold. He looked at her as if she was speaking a foreign language.

She tried to explain. "They aren't.... They need to begin—"

He silenced her with a raised hand. "Let's see what *you* can do!"

Momentarily at a loss, Joy took a deep breath and plunged in. "Excuse me...Uh...Hello!" she called out as she walked over to the team. "Could I have your attention, please!"

The Knights ignored her.

Bewildered, she turned to Coach Merlin.

With his hands on his hip and a grin on his face, he seemed to be enjoying her frustration.

She walked over to him, grabbed the whistle around his neck and blew.

The Knights stopped what they were doing.

Pleased with herself, she addressed the team. "Now then. You call this 'warming up,' don't you. Well, I think you've 'warmed up' quite enough. What I'd like you to do is execute some programs just the way you would—"

"Huh?... Execute?...Programs?... What the hell is she talkin' about?!"

Joy consulted her tablet. "Oh, uh I mean *plays*. Let's uh...*run some plays*. Okay? Like in a real game."

At the end of his rope, Kingman exploded. "What the hell do you think we've been doing?!"

"Look," Joy said, trying to keep her anger in check, "I know this isn't easy for you. It's a little strange for me, too. So I'd appreciate your cooperation."

As she headed back to the sideline command center, IQ turned to Kingman who was still watching her. "What d'ya think of our new coach?"

"She's kinda cute when she's angry."

————————

By the time Joy returned to her command center she was steaming. A burst of laughter from the field was the last straw. Angrily, she punched in a code on her console. A mischievous smile brightened her face. She bit her lip in anticipation.

On the field, the Knights did a double-take as a football player in a space-age uniform emerged from one of the hangars and trotted onto the field. His face was hidden by a black visor and he wore #34.

The Knights rode him mercilessly.

"Yo! It's The Flash!"

"It's a bird! It's a plane! It's Super Back!"

"Needs that visor to hide his ugly face!"

From the sidelines, Coach Merlin and Malibu watched #34 line up in Malibu's slot.

The trash talk from the Wrecking Crew escalated.

"This turkey's gonna get creamed!"

"Tear this mother apart!"

"Time he was introduced to the Wrecking Crew!"

Joy monitored the trash talk from her command center. The Knights' non-stop bluster was getting under her skin. Impulsively, she tapped a screen raising the setting from 1 to 3.

On the field, the ball was snapped—#34 took the handoff from Kingman and ran right through Hacksaw and the defense for a good gain. The Knights were grudgingly impressed.

Hacksaw extended a hand to help #34 to his feet.

But #34 ignored him and headed back to the huddle.

Hacksaw glared after him. "This asshole's definitely got an attitude problem! Needs to be re-educated! Taught 21st century manners!"

Pleased with herself, Joy reduced the setting to 1. On the next play #34 was gang-tackled at the line of scrimmage. Though buried at the bottom of the pile, his legs kept moving!

Joy's instruments flashed, indicating a malfunction. Acting quickly she corrected the problem.

On the field, #34's legs stopped moving and he got to his feet.

This time Meathook tried being friendly. "Way to keep those legs movin'!"

Without so much as a nod, #34 walked right past Meathook. Now the Wrecking Crew was pissed—#34 needed to be taught a lesson.

On the next play, Meathook and Hacksaw tag-teamed #34 with a vicious tackle. In the pileup a fight broke out and #34 began flailing about wildly.

The indicators on Joy's console redlined. She worked frantically to fix it.

On the field, #34's flailing suddenly stopped.

Seizing the moment, Hacksaw ripped #34's visor off! He was flabbergasted to discover glowing, pulsing circuitry where a face should have been!

"What the hell?!" Hacksaw exclaimed.

"Holy shit!!!" the Knights echoed.

27

A shaken Joy conferred with Dr. Newton outside a NAFA lecture hall, while inside the Knights were in an uproar. "They're so..." she stammered trying to explain. "I...I don't know what got into me. I...I'm so sorry...I just—"

Newton waved her apology away. To her surprise, he didn't seem upset. "It was bound to happen," he said reassuringly. "It was just a matter of time."

He took her by the shoulders and looked her in the eye. "Are you ready?" Though she dreaded the confrontation, she nodded. Newton opened the door to the lecture hall and Joy, bracing herself against the Knights' outrage, followed him in.

Newton's entrance into the hall silenced the Knights but only for a moment.

Joy looked on helplessly as the Director of NAFA was confronted by what appeared to her an angry mob.

Newton raised his hand for quiet. "Please! Let me explain! We had to *show* you first."

This unleashed another wave of outrage from the Knights, but now spiced with curses. Joy had never witnessed anything like it and feared this could turn into a riot.

Unfazed, Newton stood his ground and raised his hands once again. "Please! *Please*!!" he pleaded, looking to Coach Merlin and then to Kingman for help. "If you'll just let me, I'll explain everything."

Still in their uniforms, disgruntled Knights followed Newton and Joy into an impressive atrium. In the center of the hall surrounded by exhibits depicting the evolution of robot football, Newton began his tour of the NAFA Museum.

"That Russian Gorabachkov—"

"Gorbachev, " IQ corrected him.

"Yes. Thank you. That's where it all began."

The Knights were in no mood for a history lesson. They looked to Kingman, but he was totally focused on what Newton was saying.

"With the end of what you called the 'Cold War,' the 'arms race' quickly became a 'technology race.' While we busied ourselves building the Internet, Japan focused on becoming the undisputed leader in robotics."

"What happened to China?" Kingman asked.

"They had lots of catching up to do," Newton patiently explained. "At first their unlimited manpower held them back. Insufficient motivation. But when the 'sleeping dragon' finally woke up at the turn of the 21st century and became the cheap manufacturing center for the entire world, they began employing robots more and more. With access to the latest technologies, they copied, some might say stole, advanced robotics, especially from the Japanese. With the breakthrough in carbon nano-tube technology replacing the silicon chip...."

Seeing the glaze of confusion on the Knights' faces, Newton shifted gears. "Before the world realized it, China had become a technology leader to be reckoned with."

Newton led them over to several mural-sized screens running slideshows of old news photos. "To showcase their technology," he continued, "the Chinese unveiled a robot football team during an International Robotics Exhibition back in 2027. With Asian cunning, the Chinese figured that football was the way to challenge American technological dominance without our even realizing it. Within a few short years they even promoted robot exhibition games which toured the world."

Murmurs of disdain and disbelief arose from the Knights.

"At first people were curious," Newton explained. "After all, it was an oddity. Our media cynically labeled these exhibition games as the ultimate version of *Kick the Can*. But with typical Asian determination, the Chinese and Japanese robot performances improved every year until a robot football league, the old RFL, was launched in 2033."

While some Knights cringed and cursed, others chuckled.

"Although it began as a joke, the robot league soon attracted hardcore fans. Within a few years, their performance specs began to match those of the NFL."

There was head-shaking and eye-rolling.

"So it was inevitable," Newton pressed on, "that the robot league would challenge the NFL to a 'friendly' exhibition game."

Despite their smirks, it seemed to Joy as if some of the Knights had puffed out their chests.

"Who won?" Kingman asked.

Newton smiled patronizingly at the question's naiveté. "Naturally the NFL declined."

A chorus of "Huh?"s expressed the Knights' confusion.

"Even back then we felt it was..." Newton made a show of trying to find the right word, *"Unsportsmanlike...* even—"

"It's just plain wrong!" Coach Merlin declared.

"For humans to compete against machines," Newton summed up. "Exactly!"

A murmur of agreement spread among the Knights.

Joy watched with increasing awe as Newton conducted a master class in the politics of persuasion.

"But public opinion gradually changed and over the years—"

"How's that possible?" Coach Merlin demanded.

"Good question," Newton said with an approving nod. "A few visionary leaders believed that America could not allow other countries to control the robotics market which was quickly becoming the most important integrative technology of the world economy."

"So...?" Kingman prompted.

"So they lobbied the government and persuaded the public to develop an American robot football team to compete with the Chinese, the Japanese and German-led EU." Newton paused to let the Knights digest this. "In 2042, America decided to face up to the challenge. NAFA—the National Android Football Administration—was born. Like the old NASA, its mission was to coordinate a massive national effort, not to put a man on the moon, but to field the best robot football team in the world to showcase American technological superiority."

Newton led the Knights over to an exhibit of the first American robot football players.

"They're just a bunch of tin cans!" Hacksaw cracked, sparking the team's laughter.

"That's how everyone reacted," Newton said. "They thought it was a big joke. At first. That was nearly eighty years ago."

IQ jumped in. "I remember reading somewhere about this thing called Moore's Law. It said that computing power doubles every year, making it exponential."

"Every two years to be exact," Newton replied. "But that law referred to silicon-based chips. We're way beyond that now."

IQ was impressed, but the Knights grumbled about this digression.

Newton seemed to agree. "I'm sure most of you don't care what we make our robots out of, so let's move on."

He led them over to a chronological exhibit of early models of robot football players. "Each year NAFA unveiled new and improved models that incorporated the latest advances in technology." Like the antique exhibits in a car museum, these models were comparable to Model-T's, Packards and Duesenberg's. But later models began to resemble human players.

"How come they look so human, so life-like?" Coach Merlin asked.

"Yeah, these don't look like machines," Kingman added.

"Exactly. They were designed to give spectators the illusion of humans competing."

"Marketing," TJ cracked.

"Yes. It was also a political decision to give robot football credibility. And it's become the tradition."

Newton led the Knights over to an exhibit titled "Ultra Bowl."

"At first the American team was no match for China, Japan, or even the EU teams. But in the same way we created the Manhattan Project during World War II to build an atomic bomb, or the way we put a man on the moon, when America commits to a great goal, nothing can stop us. In just a few years the United States began to play in the Ultra Bowl."

The Knights couldn't resist—"USA! USA!"

Newton smiled. "As the audience for robot football grew, interest in human football declined."

"Man, you gotta be kidding!" Malibu spoke for the rest of the team.

"Let me explain," Newton said over the Knights' muttered disbelief. "In a last desperate attempt to compete with the increasingly popular robot games, the NFL waived the rules that had protected players in order to make the game more violent. But despite every effort by the beleaguered NFL to make human football more entertaining, attendance dropped."

Seeing the stunned expressions on the Knights' faces, Newton exuded sympathy. "I realize this may be hard for you to believe since in your time football was America's secular religion. But the interests of increasing numbers of people who believed football was too violent, and the interests of those visionaries who saw in robotics the key to America's future, combined in a powerful political movement that legislated the abolition of professional football."

In response to the Knights' confusion, Newton restated the obvious. "Hard as it may be for you to believe, by 2052 professional football played by humans was outlawed."

Some Knights were speechless, others outraged.

Over the hubbub, Newton declared, "But attitudes changed."

The Knights grew silent.

"In time people realized that this prohibition was an over-reaction to the last gasp desperation of the dying NFL's 'blood & guts' strategy. It lasted less than a decade. By 2060 a more rational view prevailed and that ridiculous law was repealed."

Some Knights muttered agreement, others sighed with relief.

"By that time," Newton added gravely like a doctor delivering bad news, "it was too late. With no audience and no TV money, people stopped playing football."

"That's impossible!" Kingman gasped.

"It's not the first time in history," Newton replied. "I'm sure the mighty Romans expected their gladiators to still be fighting to the death today."

As the stunned Knights followed Newton out of the museum, a "tour guide's" voice summed up: "In the last few decades of the 21st century, the Ultra Bowl has become the ultimate technological battleground in the economic wars being waged between nations. In less than fifty years, the Ultra Bowl has gone from a freak sideshow spectacle to the preeminent world event that determines the economic and geopolitical balance of power. NAFA is proud to lead the United States effort to..."

Back in the lecture hall, the Knights confronted Newton.

"I don't want my team playing against some damned machines," Coach Merlin declared.

"Yeah," Hacksaw agreed, "we're not too crazy about playin' a bunch of tin cans!"

"They're not *tin cans* as you saw for yourselves," Newton reminded them.

Coach Merlin waxed philosophically. "Hell, we lost the big one. It's tough. But there'll be other games, other—"

"You're wrong!" Newton was vehement. "One game is all it would take. Believe me. Until now the games have always been close. We've lost a few. But the point spread has always been small. If, for the first time, we lose the Ultra Bowl by a big margin—"

"You mean a blowout?" IQ interjected. "Say 45 - 0?"

"Exactly! Then American robotics technology will become worthless overnight."

"You make it sound like it's the end of the world," Kingman said.

"In a way it would be." There was no mistaking the gravity in his voice. "Don't forget, our team was *sabotaged*," he said, playing the patriot card. "We were attacked. It may have been the first battle of a cyber war. Who knows what those responsible ultimately want to achieve?"

Newton could see from the expressions on the Knights' faces that they were being swayed. The consummate manipulator, he left the choice in their hands. "It's your decision."

In the silence that followed he shifted gears.

"I'd hoped you'd rise to the challenge," he said with a mournful sigh. "We've always believed that our football legends were special. Real heroes. Perhaps we were wrong."

Newton walked with Joy to the door. Before exiting, he turned and floated a thinly veiled threat. "If you entertain any hope of returning to your previous lives, I remind you that continued funding for time-travel research depends on an Ultra Bowl victory."

Alone in the lecture hall, the Knights grew silent as their predicament sunk in. Several minutes passed as they digested all they'd seen and heard, Finally, Kingman stood and tried to rally his team. "Hell, we just have to think of it as a game of *kick the can!*"

28

The mood in the Knights' locker room was different than it had been earlier. They'd suited up on autopilot, but getting out of their uniforms was anything but routine.

The men were stunned; they seemed lost. Some sat in front of their lockers staring off into space, as if they'd forgotten how to undo their shoulder pads. While others wandered into the showers still half-dressed.

Their on-field bluster gone, they were coming to grips with what they'd experienced on the practice field, what they'd heard at the NAFA Museum, but mostly with the idea of playing against robots in the Ultra Bowl.

"We're like fucking dinosaurs!"

"Welcome to Jurassic Park."

"Machines? It's..."

"Inconceivable!"

"*Immoral* to play against machines!"

"Where's the thrill of victory and the agony of defeat?"

"What kind of world is it where people don't play football?"

"Not a world I want to live in!"

A mournful silence settled over them. In some ways they were as devastated as they'd been around the bonfire when they'd grieved the loss of their old lives. Now they experienced another kind of death—a loss of meaning. What did it mean to be the best, if people no longer valued what you did?

Hacksaw suddenly erupted in a violent outburst of fury, cursing and pounding his locker with his helmet.

"That's enough!" Coach Merlin ordered, trying to contain the violence before it spread to the rest of his players.

Hacksaw threw his helmet on the floor and slumped down in front of his locker.

Coach Merlin walked over to him and put a reassuring hand on his shoulder. "I understand your anger," he began as more Knights gathered around. "It's not a game if humans play machines. The game was never really about the points...or even who won and who lost. Deep down, it was always about heart, spirit. It was a way to find out what we're made of."

Youngblood jumped in. "Remember that news we saw about protests by anti-robot terrorists?"

"Maybe we're playing for the wrong side?" Reggie wondered.

"Yeah," TJ agreed, "and what a coincidence we show up just in time to save their asses in their damned Ultra Bowl."

"Coincidence? I don't think so," Meathook muttered.

"Why not?" Kingman, wearing a towel around his waist after showering, joined the conversation. Unlike the other Knights, he didn't seem fazed by the idea of playing robots.

"Hey Duke," Reggie asked, "you really want to play against these machines?"

"If that's how they do things now, why not? A game's a game."

"But it's not right," Hacksaw declared, "it's—"

"The way it is!" Kingman didn't want to hear anything that might jeopardize the Knights playing another game and his chance at redemption.

"Don't you want to send these hunks of metal to the scrap heap where they belong?" he taunted. "I don't know about you, but I want to show this lunatic world that machines can't compete with—"

"You really think our being here is a coincidence?" TJ demanded.

"Maybe not," Kingman replied. "But it could also be fate."

"Huh?" some of the Knights muttered.

"Yeah," Kingman said, liking the sound of it, "Kinda like destiny."

PART V

The Blind Awakener

29

IQ got acquainted with his new accommodations at the NAFA dorm by taking his smart-room for a spin.

"Lights!" he commanded. They faded up. "How about a bath?" Hearing the sound of water running, he grinned. "Open the window."

A computer-generated voice sounding like a deferential butler stated, "I'm sorry. In order to maintain a controlled environment, the windows cannot be opened. Would you like the temperature changed?"

"Typical," he sighed.

"Does that mean cooler?" the deferential voice asked. "Or warmer?"

He had enough. "Forget it. And stop the bath." When he heard the water shut off, he muttered, "I gotta get out of here." At the door, he searched for a knob. There was none! Exasperated, he groaned, "Now how the hell am I supposed to open the goddamned door?!"

The door slid open.

Suddenly, a strange-looking dog hurried past him down the hall. Curious, he followed it to a lounge that resembled a video game arcade. Hunched over one of the machines was a chubby, freckle-faced, 12 year-old boy.

IQ watched in astonishment as the dog went over to him and said, "Joy is looking for you."

Totally engrossed, the boy whined, "Why is it always at the 7th level?"

"Insufficient information," the dog replied. "Rephrase the question."

IQ suddenly understood—"It's a *robot!*"

Startled, the boy looked up and saw a dumbfounded IQ standing in the doorway. "Who're you?" he asked, a wary expression clouding his face.

IQ walked into the lounge. "You can call me IQ."

"IQ?" the boy repeated. "That's a weird name."

"Yeah, I guess so," IQ agreed. "What's yours?"

The boy hesitated—he wasn't used to talking to strangers. "Uh...Fig," he finally answered.

"Fig, huh? That's a little weird, too. Fig what?"

The boy introduced himself with an obvious sense of pride. "Fig *Newton!*"

IQ burst out laughing.

Fig didn't get the joke and didn't like being laughed at. Head down, he hurried past IQ and left the lounge with the robot dog at his heels.

"Hey!... Wait!" IQ called out to the boy. "I'm sorry. I didn't mean... It's just such a...."

Fig had already disappeared down the hall.

Alone, IQ decided to investigate this strange game room. He approached the console Fig had been at. It activated. The array of virtual screens and controls was daunting. A gamer himself, IQ was fascinated. He tried to play, but it was the strangest game he'd ever encountered —incredibly fast and complex, way beyond him.

30

In her lab, Joy huddled over multiple screens studying the Knights' performance. She wasn't pleased with the results. She tried various simulations, continually tweaking the algorithms, but nothing helped. Confronted by what seemed to be an impossible task, she reached for her bag and withdrew a pill dispenser. Popping a few pills in her mouth, she closed her eyes in anticipation of their calming effect.

An alert startled her—a visitor had entered the lab. Her irritation vanished the moment she saw the robot dog. Sure enough, an out-of-breath Fig was right behind.

She got up to greet him. "Hi, stranger!"

When she reached out to hug him, he shrank from her the way only a young boy can. Noticing him huffing and puffing, she frowned. "Maybe you ought to start doing some exercise."

"What for?"

She glanced at the robot dog. "So you can keep up with your inventions."

Annoyed, he rolled his eyes. "Why'd you send for me?"

"Is it a crime to want to *see* you?" Realizing she'd played the guilt card, she backed off. "How's the food at the dorms? You okay there?"

"You know, I'm not a kid anymore."

"Well, after all this is over, like it or not, you're moving back home with me. And we're going to take a trip together. Just the two of us. Like a real brother and sister. Okay?"

Fig wasn't paying attention to what she said because he was riveted by the "antique" NFL football games playing on several screens. Puzzled, he wondered, "Why would anyone want to play football? Were people really that primitive a hundred years ago?"

"Things were different then."

While she shut down the lab, Fig studied the screens on which the Knights' versus the robots' performance analytics were displayed. "Are they really gonna play?" he asked in disbelief,

She sighed—Fig didn't need to know about this.

"Holy Iaccoca!" he exclaimed, knowing what his sister's sigh meant. "Are they *crazy*?!"

Since the cat was out of the bag, she tried to answer his question. "They think they're the best in the world. And maybe once they were."

As Joy and Fig floated tree-top level across the NAFA campus in an anti-gravity vehicle resembling a golf cart, Joy thought about her earlier meeting with Newton.

She'd told her uncle that she wouldn't be separated from her brother by a quarantine. He'd protested—Fig posed a security risk. "He's a child!" she'd countered. Newton had been adamant. So Joy had given him an ultimatum. "If you want me to 'coach' these humans, those are my conditions." Though displeased, Newton had no choice. "Alright," he relented. "But you'll assume full responsibility. And I strongly suggest you limit any contact."

Once Joy and Fig landed on the lawn in front of Fig's dorm, they sat in silence for a moment savoring the twilight.

Finally Joy turned to Fig. "So you'll keep your distance?"

"Uhuh."

"Uncle Devlin says it's crucial they think they can win. So don't go saying anything that might make them think they can't."

"Who me?"

"You know how important this is."

"I know."

"Promise me."

"I promise."

Joy held out her pinky.

Fig immediately hooked pinkies to reassure her.

She flashed her kid brother a big smile, then leaned over to hug him.

Too late—he'd already jumped out and was running to his dorm.

31

Joy stared out the window of her apartment. Though the sky was filled with stars, she didn't see them. She was also oblivious of the virtual screens surrounding her that played and analyzed old broadcasts of New York Knights' games.

"Why not?" she finally murmured. "Why the hell not!?!" she repeated with growing conviction. "Phone Dr. Noel Christianson!"

The Knights' games paused as Christianson's answering message began to play on her wall screen.

"Damn!" she muttered, realizing he wasn't picking up.

"I'm unavailable for the moment," Christianson said, standing among a group of naked mannequins.

The image startled Joy.

"If you really want to find me," Christianson's message concluded, "you have to return to the Garden of Eden."

Joy's conviction evaporated.

———

A "taxi" craft touched down on a seedy, rain-soaked street by the waterfront. Joy got out, looked around and shuddered. Compared to the manicured order of NAFA, she'd landed on another planet. Steeling herself, she took a deep breath and headed for the flashing antique neon sign—"Garden of Eden."

Inside, Joy scanned the dingy, dimly-lit bar looking for Christianson. She'd lived a pretty sheltered life within the sterile confines of NAFA, and wasn't prepared for the chaos, commotion and odd assortment of characters she now confronted. Part of her wanted to leave, but she fought her fear, made her way to the bar and tried to get the bartender's attention.

"What a surprise!" someone called out from behind her.

She spun around to find a very drunken Christianson, drink in hand, approaching her. "Dr. Christianson!" she exclaimed, feigning surprise but inwardly relieved. "Uh... What are *you* doing here?"

Christianson raised his glass. "I had a shitty day!" He shot her a quizzical look. "What's *your* excuse?"

"Oh uh...me, too!"

"Then join me!" As he drunkenly steered her over to his table, she stumbled. In the dim light, the floor seemed to be moving beneath her. She looked closer and gasped—snakes slithered across it.

Christianson laughed. "They're harmless," he reassured her. "Quite an ambience, huh?"

Seated at last in a booth, her legs protectively curled up beneath her, Joy was mesmerized by the snake coiling on the chandelier above. "This is a very strange place."

Christianson wasn't listening, he was watching a nearby virtual screen that played the Blind Awakener's subversive message.

Though Joy felt guilty for having listened to his anti-robot diatribe the other night, there was something compelling about this blind terrorist leader that she couldn't explain. Following Christianson's lead, she listened to more of what he had to say.

"The seeds were sown a hundred years ago," he said, "when our work world became 24/7. We no longer lived in a human world of night and day, we had stepped into a perpetual machine world and were on our way to a robotic world.

"Back then you could see lovers walking along beautiful beaches and, rather than savoring the moment and each other, they were glued instead to their digital devices, which they called *smartphones*.

"It was common back then for a family to be sitting around the dinner table, each fixated on his device, oblivious of those around him. All those screens mirrored back to us a kaleidoscope of enchanting and fascinating reflections. We were being hypnotized. We became addicted. Where religion had once been called the opiate of the masses, now our digital reflections became our drug of choice.

"While we were seduced with the illusion and convenience of having a world in our hands, we didn't realize that we were being shackled by a new and invisible slavery. While we constantly monitored it, it monitored us. Soon we began to actually wear our shackles on our wrists and called them *smart* watches.

"People began to spend more time with their digital devices than with the flesh and blood people in their lives. We sensed something unhealthy, even dangerous about this new world. Some of the most popular stories of that time were about vampires and zombies, warning us that our lifeblood was being sucked out of us, that we were becoming the disembodied zombies, the walking dead, that haunted our collective dreams. But we were in thrall to our devices and didn't listen.

"The Ancients were wiser than we give them credit. They talked about a Fall caused by humans taking a bite out of a forbidden apple. We laugh at the notion. Is it irony or destiny that an image of a bitten apple is emblazoned on so many of the devices that became our invisible masters?"

Christianson, who'd been listening with rapt attention to the Blind Awakener's message, suddenly remembered Joy sitting across from him.

"The old Garden of Eden," he declared. "Maybe *paradise* is just another word for *prison*. What do you think? Maybe we weren't thrown out. Maybe we escaped!" Through a drunken haze he suddenly remembered his manners. "Sorry. What would you like to drink?"

Disoriented by both the place and the Blind Awakener's message, Joy muttered, "Vita Water would be fine."

Christianson hailed a passing waitress. "One Vita Water, please. And I'll have another. Make it a double."

Joy stared at the waitress as if she'd seen a ghost.

"*Real* waitresses!" Christianson confirmed. "Quaint, isn't it!" He sipped his drink. "So what brings the pride of NAFA to a place like this?"

Joy hesitated—she was having second thoughts about telling him.

"Well...?" Christianson coaxed. "We all have our secrets." He took another long drink emptying his glass.

"Why do *you* come here?"

Christianson held up his empty glass and looked at her through it. "I'm looking for *real* people!" His speech was thick, almost slurred. "Had your tits done yet?" He reached out across the table as if to squeeze her breast.

Appalled, she smacked his hand away. "How dare you!"

Christianson grew contrite. "Sorry. Just call me Diogenes. That old Greek looked everywhere for an honest man. All I'm trying to find is a pair of real tits! And when I do, I'll get down on my knees and—"

"You're *drunk*!"

"Thank God!"

"You're—"

The waitress brought their drinks.

Once they were alone, Christianson didn't waste any time knocking back his freshened drink.

Joy watched him with growing revulsion.

"Don't look at me like that," he said defensively. "Oh, I was a true believer. Just like you! Blessed to be living in our brave new world! Humanity liberated from toil!" He raised his glass. "To Robotopia! To Paradise!" He drank.

Meanwhile, Joy couldn't take her eyes off the slithering and coiling snakes.

Noting her fascination, he continued his drunken rant. "But there's a snake in the garden! See, the more the robots do, the less time we have! Funny! They were supposed to *give* us time! Truth is they've *stolen* our time! We're like hamsters on a treadmill of our own making. Faster and faster it goes! And as hard as we try, we can't keep up!"

"So it's true!" she said. "You're anti-robot!"

Christianson warmed to his confession. "I couldn't keep up! There's only one cure. You know about the rehabs? They make you live in 'primitive' conditions. No robots! You live by the old 'sweat of your brow!' It's tough! But it works! Cause you start bitching about the drudgery and the hard work and you're cured!"

He took another drink. "Problem is, it can't last. You come back to civilization and the next thing you know, you're back in paradise, back on the treadmill to nowhere!"

"Is that why you drink?" she asked, a hint of sympathy in her voice.

He ignored the question. Instead, he became the prosecutor. "How many pills do *you* take a day? 20? 50? 100?"

Joy didn't like being interrogated and shifted in her seat as if she was about to get up and leave.

Christianson backed off. "At the top of my form I was doing over 100 pills a day—vitamins, catalysts, blockers, food substitutes, mood-controllers, brain enhancers, nano-enzymes... You name it!"

"You didn't answer my question."

"Why do I drink?" Christianson asked rhetorically. As if needing to remind himself before he could answer, he downed the rest of his drink "If you live in a so-called paradise which is really a prison, maybe your vice is really a virtue and the means to your salvation." Seeing Joy's confusion, he tried to translate. "It's my protest! It unplugs me! It—!"

"But it's no good for you!" she insisted.

"*Exactly!*" Christianson declared, pleased that he'd finally gotten through to her. "It's messy. It makes me sick. Gives me godawful hangovers! It *hurts!*"

Joy shook her head. "I still don't understand..."

Christianson grabbed her bag and pulled out her automatic pill dispenser. "We prayed for wonder drugs. Be careful what you wish for. These babies are so wonderful you can take as many as you want. And there's no pain, no side effects to warn us—"

"About *what*?!" She took her pill dispenser back.

"That we're turning ourselves into machines!"

She stared at him. "You're mad! You're not only a masochist, you're paranoid!"

"First it was a robot in every home," he said, building up a head of steam. "And then a personal robot for everyone. Life, Liberty and your own mechanical slave. Isn't it ironic? The treasure at the end of our great technological rainbow is a repackaged barbarism! *Slavery!*"

"Slavery!?" she rolled her eyes. "You need help."

"We all do! Cause the joke's on us. We're so damned helpless, so dependent on our robots, we can't survive without them! So now who's the master and who's the slave?!"

"You're starting to sound like that crazy man in his cave."

"In the land of the blind," he muttered into his empty glass, "the one-eyed man is king."

Though confused, Joy remembered why she wanted to meet Christianson in the first place. "If that's how you feel, why do you work in bionics?"

He looked up at her. As he spoke, his eyes lit up. "If humans could be improved enough, we could compete with robots and maybe win back our freedom." He ran his hands through his tangled red hair. His face flushed, his brow beaded with sweat, and his bloodshot eyes closed for a moment as if he dozed off.

Joy's revulsion was replaced by pity.

When he finally opened his eyes, he saw Joy studying him. "You think I'm crazy, don't you."

She didn't answer. She didn't have to.

He looked away. "I'd rather waste my life on a noble failure, than put another brick in the wall."

"What?"

"Pink Floyd." Seeing her confusion, he explained, "Classical music. An eccentricity of mine. Among others." Suddenly, he lurched forward, his hand covering his mouth. "I'm gonna be sick!" he groaned, then ran to the bathroom.

For a moment Joy sat there stunned, trying to digest all she'd seen and heard. Finally, she muttered to an absent Christianson, "Have you got a surprise coming!"

Stepping gingerly over the slithering snakes, Joy left the Garden of Eden.

32

As the Knights' offense ran pass plays on the NAFA practice field, IQ noticed Fig watching from the sidelines. He yelled to Kingman, "Hit me with a sideline!"

Kingman nodded.

IQ ran the pass pattern in Fig's direction. Kingman's pass was slightly overthrown. IQ leapt and made an amazing catch landing at Fig's feet. Clutching the football triumphantly, he looked up at Fig expecting to be deluged with compliments.

"Can't jump very high, can you?" the boy said.

A bewildered IQ watched him walk away.

Further down the field, the Wrecking Crew—in the middle of their defensive drills—became aware of the chubby kid watching them from the sideline. A few of the Crew tried to be friendly, but the kid was totally unresponsive.

"Kids these days are really weird!" Meathook muttered.

Hacksaw had another take. "He's just star struck." Turning to Fig, he called out, "Hey kid, want an autograph?"

"What for?"

Hacksaw told the Wrecking Crew. "That kid gives me the creeps!"

Backup quarterback, Lance Youngblood, was warming up his arm when he saw Fig approach. He smiled. "Hey kid, here you go..." he said, tossing Fig a short, gentle pass.

To Youngblood's surprise, the boy jumped out of the way and just kept going.

During a break in practice, Smoke dealt some 3-Card Monte to a group of Knights. "Keep your eye on the Queen," he rapped, "she's got the green."

With speed and finesse, he slid three cards face down around and around each other. When he finished shuffling them, he turned one over to reveal the Queen of Hearts. His demonstration done, he turned the Queen face down again, and slid the cards round and around to confuse his audience.

No matter how many times the Knights tried, they couldn't pick the Queen. None of them, including IQ, could beat Smoke at his shell game. Again and again, he hustled them.

Fig walked over to see what all the fuss was about.

"Find the Red Queen and get the green!" Smoke chanted as he slid the cards past each other. "Where is she? Where's that Lady?" Seeing Fig, he taunted him. "Think you can find her, kid?"

Fig pointed to a card. "That one."

Smoke turned the card over—the Red Queen!

"Beginner's luck," Smoke muttered. "Let's see you do it again, kid."

Smoke shuffled and Fig picked the Queen again!

The Knights, glad to see somebody beat Smoke, began rooting for the kid.

Smoke rubbed his hands together and shuffled the cards once more.

Fig picked the Queen for a third time!

Smoke did a slow burn.

IQ, on the other hand, was impressed.

33

Joy hurried down the hall, her eyes darting about in search of something. Turning a corner, she was relieved to see Coach Merlin. As she approached him, she flashed a big smile trying to be friendly. "I guess this is where they get ready," she said, indicating the door behind him.

He nodded. "We call it a *locker room*."

"I...uh...was just checking to see where it was. It's new. I... We...uh...haven't used a *locker room* before."

"I don't suppose you have," he replied dryly.

Sensing his hostility, she tried a little flattery. "I've done some research. Your record is very impressive. They say you're the best!"

His reserve began to melt. "We'll see, won't we."

"I wonder if I could ask you a question?" Though her tone was matter-of-fact, her blue eyes beseeched him.

Unable to resist the plea of a lady in distress, he relented. "Sure...Why not."

"I haven't much experience with—"

"Humans?"

She ignored his dig and nodded. "How can I get your team to pay attention to me?"

"Start thinking about them as *your* team."

"Okay. That's good. So how can I get *my* players to listen to me?"

He gave her shorts-and-tank-top "coach" outfit an exaggerated once-over. "Try dressing differently."

She seemed puzzled.

"They're *men!*" he said. "Not machines."

"Oh." Suddenly understanding, she blushed.

He found her naiveté strange. "You have some experience with men, I presume."

"Oh *sure!*" Embarrassed, she wanted to end their conversation but there was more she needed to know. "Can I ask you something else?"

Coach Merlin nodded wearily.

Joy girded herself for one final question. "You may not believe it, but I do understand the game. What I need help with is how to motivate your, I mean my—"

"Like I said," he interrupted, "you've been working with robots. They're *machines*. They have no heart! You may understand the game—the strategy, tactics, the metrics and the moves. But you haven't got a clue how to inspire, motivate and lead—"

"I know!" she agreed. "I realize that. That's why I need—"

"To tap into their greatness!" He paused for a moment. "I really don't know what the equivalent would be for a machine?"

"Uh...there is none."

"Of course not. Humans play games as an excuse—"

"Why? For what?"

"To see what we're made of!"

"Fascinating!" she murmured. "Thank you."

She was about to leave when he grabbed her arm. "Maybe now you'll help me."

"Sure," she replied, though she wasn't nearly as sure as she sounded.

He looked down the hall and, seeing they were alone, whispered to her, "What's really going on? Newton has us quarantined. We're totally in the dark. There's more than we're being told. Much more. Tell me. I need to know."

She started to back away. "I'm sorry. I...I can't. I—"

He was insistent. "I have to protect these men. They're my players, they're like my—"

She pulled her arm away. "I have to go."

He pressed her. "How good are these robots?"

"You...uh...saw for yourself," she said in a shaky voice.

"My first responsibility isn't winning, it's *protecting* my players. I have to know what they're up against."

She backed away. "I can only answer your questions on a *need-to-know*."

"Dammit, I *need to know*!" he hissed.

She looked away. "I'm sorry."

Frustrated, he headed back to the locker room muttering to himself, "If only there were some special equipment they could use...." He held the locker room door open for her. "Would you like to see it for yourself?"

But she was already gone.

34

Wearing her new outfit—jeans and a sweatshirt—Joy monitored the Knights' afternoon practice from her sideline command center. She'd been pleased by the more conservative image she saw in the mirror, but now she was increasingly dismayed by the Knights' performance specs she saw on her screens.

IQ ran a pass pattern toward the sideline, dove for and missed Kingman's slightly overthrown pass.

"You should've caught that!" Joy yelled, venting her frustration on him. "Can't you run faster?! Is that as high as you can jump?!"

Malibu had been trying to keep a straight face when suddenly Joy turned to the All-Pro back and let him have it, too. "You have to break those tackles! According to my readings the force per square inch isn't...that great!"

Kingman just stared at the ground while Joy bawled him out for that overthrown pass. "You're taking too long to—"

"Never had any problems before," he muttered, trying to contain himself.

Meanwhile, some Knights began mimicking Joy behind her back. Their schoolboy antics quickly reduced everyone, even Kingman, to fits of laughter.

For Joy, that was the last straw. She stormed off.

By the time she arrived at her sideline command center, she'd decided to teach those "cretins" a lesson. She punched in some codes and a hangar door on the opposite side of the field opened. A team of robots dressed like #34 ran onto the field.

Hacksaw announced almost gleefully, "Time to play kick the can!"

———————

As the robots lined up on defense, Reggie cracked, "Anybody got an oil can?"

At her console, Joy lowered the robots' settings to 1.

On their first play, the Knights offense steamrolled over the robots as Malibu ran for an easy touchdown. The Knights whooped and hollered while Malibu did a victory dance in the end zone.

On the next series of plays, the Knights taunted the robots mercilessly.

"Nothing sweeter than the sound of bearings grinding!"

"What's a matter, got a stick up your hydraulics?!"

"Time for an overhaul, Tin Man!"

Even Coach Merlin got into the act with a sideline aside to Joy. "Maybe you could use 'em for scrap metal!"

That did it! Joy increased the robots' settings to 3.

Newton arrived anxious to observe the Knights' practice and was pleased to see them acting so confident.

On the next play, the robot defense tore through the Knights' offensive line and gang tackled Malibu for a big loss! The Knights were stunned.

As Newton hurried to Joy's command center, he yelled encouragement to the team. "Even machines can get lucky!"

While the Knights huddled for the next play, Newton, without a word to Joy, lowered the robots' settings to 1.

Joy began to apologize. "I'm sorry. I don't know what came over me. I just find them so...so difficult, so conceited!...so...!!"

Newton wasn't listening. He was on his way to confer with Coach Merlin.

On the next play, Kingman handed off to Malibu who slashed his way through the robot defense for another easy score.

Newton patted Coach Merlin on the back. "You've got a great team there!"

Pleased, Coach Merlin blew his whistle ending practice.

As the Knights left the field, Newton returned to Joy.

She was contrite. "I'm sorry, I just can't seem to—"

"There's no need," he said, waving off her apology. "I know it's difficult for you, but you mustn't be plagued by doubts. I have complete confidence in you."

While Newton and Joy walked off the field, he offered her some advice. "Above all, give them hope. It's an essential factor in human performance. Play on their egos, their vanity. Use psychology or whatever you think will work. They must believe they can win! I would focus on the quarterback, Kingman."

Joy shook her head. "But he's so—!"

"He's their leader," Newton reminded her. "Whichever way he goes, the rest will follow."

35

In their locker room, the Knights continued having a good time at Joy's expense.

"Can't you break those tackles?" Reggie mimicked in a high-pitched voice. "According to my calculations the force per square inch isn't enough to break a fart!"

The team roared in laughter.

Suddenly Joy, full of renewed determination, rushed in. Confronted by so many semi-naked male bodies, she stopped dead in her tracks, the wind knocked out of her sails.

"I uh..." Embarrassed, she averted her eyes and stared at the floor.

Malibu feigned curiosity. "Hey, haven't you ever seen a robot's...uh...whaddaya call it?"

Another roar of laughter.

As Joy rushed out, she said, "Tell Kingman I want to see him in Theater C! Right away!"

A moment later, Kingman, a towel wrapped around his waist, returned from the showers. The Knights couldn't wait to tell him the news.

"Teacher wants you to stay after school," TJ ribbed him.

Malibu piled on. "And we thought she didn't like what she saw!"

36

Joy hurried down the hall fighting back tears. On the way to Theater C, she passed Newton's office. Loud voices could be heard inside. She stopped and listened.

"Misguided idealists like you just never learn," an angry Newton lectured Dr. Christianson.

She peeked in and saw Christianson flanked by two security guards.

"All the high-sounding ideals in the world," Newton continued, "are no match against power. Take your pick. The Greeks and their philosophy? No match for mighty

Rome! The grandeur of the Incas? The Aztecs? Didn't impress the Conquistadors!"

Christianson was defiant. "Re-read your history, Newton. Power without ideals never lasts. There've been ideals and ideas which have toppled the greatest powers on earth. Take your mighty Rome—"

"I'm tired of fencing with you, Christianson. You'll get your pathetic research back when I say so. And if you're caught violating the quarantine again, I'll have you arrested!" He let his threat sink in, then added, "I don't care if you're on the Board. *I'm* the Director. I give the orders." With a nod to the guards—"Escort Dr. Christianson off the grounds. Immediately."

Shocked, Joy backed away and hurried off.

37

Dressed, Kingman combed his hair in the locker room mirror with exaggerated care as his teammates looked on.

"Gotta admit," Reggie said, "she's the best looking piece of...uh *coach* I've ever had."

This elicited catcalls from some of the Knights.

Kingman checked himself in the mirror one last time as if he was about to go on a hot date. Pleased, he headed for the door. "Maybe I can show *her* a thing or two!"

All hell broke loose—the betting was fast and furious. Will Kingman seduce her?

38

Fig Newton, IQ repeated to himself. He'd laughed when he'd first heard his funny name, but now realized that the kid must be connected with the NAFA Director. So he wandered around the dorm, hoping he'd run into Fig again. Maybe he could get some information.

When he arrived at the "game room" lounge, he was delighted to find Fig inside. This time the kid wasn't playing one of those machines. Instead, he was trying, rather awkwardly, to deal a 3-Card Monte.

Amused, IQ watched from the doorway and finally cleared his throat.

Startled, Fig put the cards away and turned to one of the "game" machines which instantly activated.

"Hey there..." IQ said as he walked in. "I was good at video games in my day, but these are something else."

"They're *not* 'games'," Fig corrected. "They're mentastics."

IQ tried to decipher. *"Brain* workouts?"

Fig kept "playing" as he explained, "They increase speed, concentration...*everything!*"

IQ wondered aloud, "What about the body?"

"Huh?" Fig muttered.

"You know, building muscles... Not for *thinking,* but for *doing* things."

Fig was dumbfounded. "That's what robots are for!"

"Really." IQ pulled a coin out of his pocket and began rolling it across the back of his hand.

Fig was quickly distracted by IQ's sleight-of-hand.

IQ suddenly palmed a deck of cards and did some fancy shuffling.

Fig stopped playing to watch.

IQ fanned the deck. "Pick a card! Any card."

Intrigued, Fig picked an Ace of Spades.

Like any good magician, IQ made a big deal out of invoking his "psychic powers." Finally, he announced, "Ace of Spades!"

"How'd you do that?" Fig marveled.

IQ smiled—Fig was hooked.

39

Kingman stood in the middle of an empty cavernous room—a simulation lab known as Theater C. His body language said it all—*What the hell is going on? And what am I doing here?*

On the far side of the room, Joy manned an impressive array of screens. At her command an incredible transformation took place—a life-size holographic simulation of a robot football game filled the room turning Theater C into a virtual stadium. Joy was careful to use older models, similar to the robots Kingman was familiar with. The two robot teams were poised on the line of scrimmage waiting for the ball to be snapped.

Kingman was impressed. And a little intimidated.

Joy sensed his hesitation. "Go ahead," she coaxed.

He took his position somewhat tentatively behind the virtual robot center.

"Amazing!" he muttered.

"Ready?" Joy asked.

"Ready."

Suddenly she launched a new defensive lineup to confront Kingman, then counted the seconds. Meanwhile, her computer instantly listed ten offensive plays that would counter the new defense. Under her breath, she implored, "Come on!..."

Finally, Kingman called an audible. "25 counter trap."

She shook her head in frustration—it was 9th out of the 10 most effective plays against that defense.

"Great!" she lied.

Kingman was pleased with himself. "What other tricks you got?"

Trying to be tactful, she added, "But you need to speed it up. We've got to work on that."

She launched a new defense. Again the computer listed 10 countering offensive plays in order of their effectiveness.

Seconds later, Kingman called out his audible. It was 7th.

Joy hid her concern. "Maybe I could radio in plays."

Bored with the drill, Kingman walked off the holographic field. "Don't you know I'm famous for reading defenses," he boasted as he approached her.

"These robot defenses are probably quite different than the ones you're used to," she said as she continued making adjustments at her console.

He leaned over and whispered seductively in her ear, "I wish I could read *your* defenses."

Startled, she got up and moved away, activating a light "chalk board" on which she began diagramming plays. "Uh...Robot football relies primarily on what you call the 'power game'." She was clearly uncomfortable. "There's...uh...not much improvisation."

He pursued her. "How well can *you* improvise?"

She tried to ignore him. "And there's not nearly as much blitzing as you're used to—"

"You're very beautiful."

Though rattled, she tried to hide it. "Robots can instantaneously compute the statistical probability of—"

"Can your robots do this?" He reached out and gently caressed her cheek.

Shocked, she backed away. "What are you *doing*?!"

He took her by the shoulders. "How do *you* defend against this kind of pass?"

She was stunned, speechless, prey in a predator's grasp.

He bent slowly to kiss her. Her eyes closed. Their lips met.

After a moment, he pulled away and looked at her in astonishment.

Her eyes remained closed, her mouth pursed, almost child-like.

He couldn't believe it—she didn't know how to kiss!

Joy's eyes opened. She saw him staring at her. Unnerved, she blurted, "I have to go!" and rushed out.

Kingman was stunned. Then he gathered his wits and chased after her.

40

Fighting back tears, Joy hurried home through the manicured gardens of the NAFA campus. The evening air acted like a tonic—she felt as if she'd just woken from a bad dream.

Until Kingman caught up with her.

Joy's pace didn't slow. She wouldn't even look at him. He tried to apologize. "Hey, I didn't mean... I mean, I did, but I didn't want to upset you. I'm sorry. I...I didn't know...."

He stopped.

Without so much as a glance, she continued on her way.

He called after her. "I said I'm *sorry!*"

She kept going.

He watched her, unsure what to do. Then, with a helpless shrug, he ran after her.

––––––––––––––

Fascinated by the décor of Joy's apartment, Kingman stared at the glowing, translucent, now empty, life-sized pod.

Meanwhile, Joy took refuge in the bathroom where she gulped down a handful of pills to calm herself. When she finally emerged, she remembered her manners. "Would you uh...like something to drink?"

"No, thanks," he said with a grin. "I'm in training, coach. Remember?"

She was too rattled to get his joke. In fact, she was so uncomfortable, she poured herself a stiff drink. Then downed it.

Not wanting to upset her any further, Kingman remained silent and kept his distance.

Fortified, Joy heaved a big sigh. She needed to get something off her chest. "Uh...I...uh want to explain—"

"Hey, there's nothing to explain."

"We...I'm..." She shook her head in frustration. "It's not easy for me to talk about." She poured and downed another stiff drink, then willed herself to get to the point. "I suppose you've never heard of Erotics."

He shook his head "No."

She rolled her eyes. "Of course not." Exasperated with herself, she began to pace, as if silently rehearsing what she wanted say. Finally, she sat down on the couch.

Slowly, as if approaching a frightened animal, Kingman sat down in a nearby chair. His body language unthreatening and his intense focus indicated, *I'm all ears.*

She took a deep breath. "It started during the STD Plague back in the late '20's. Sex became so dangerous, digital 'sex aids' were developed. They were called Erotics. A kind of—"

"Robot sex?"

She nodded sheepishly.

"Holy shit!" He couldn't conceal his surprise, nor his distaste.

"You don't understand!" she defended herself. "You don't know what it was like!"

"I'm getting the picture."

"*You* had vibrators!"

"Yeah, but—"

"Same principle!" she said. "Only more sophisticated!"

"But these Erotics were way before your time," he pointed out.

"It became...uh...fashionable," she tried to explain.

"Huh?"

"Uh...hip...cool...awesome...you know."

"I get it. So once you go erotic, or should I say *robotic*, you don't go back."

"Why are you making this so difficult," she groaned. "It's just the way things were...*are*."

He tried to be more sympathetic and confided, "I like a little kink, too."

Disturbed by his innuendo, she tried to explain, "Erotics are programmed to uh...stimulate you just like..." She was too embarrassed to go on.

"Jesus!" he exclaimed, feigning outrage. "What's the world *coming* to?!" he joked. But his pun was lost on her.

Feeling as if she was on trial defending herself and her world, she made her closing argument. "By the time STD's were finally eradicated, Erotics had become a way of life...till you get married."

Kingman couldn't believe it—"You mean you...?"

Unable to look him in the eye, she shook her head. "No."

"Never?"

She looked away.

Despite his shock, Kingman tried to lighten the mood. "Well, my daddy always used to say," he drawled, *"Son, there's nothing like travel, especially time travel, to broaden your horizons."*

Joy looked at him—a hint of a smile broke through the upset that had clouded her expression.

Kingman seized the opportunity and called an audible. As if meeting her for the first time, he introduced himself. "My friends call me Duke. Mind if I call you Joy?"

Her body language softened. "Joy...Yes...of course."

With exaggerated formality, he offered his hand. "Pleasure to meet you."

She shook his hand. "Joy Newton, the pleasure is mine." Indeed. His touch warmed her entire body.

"Kind of strange, you know," he said, somewhat baffled. "I wouldn't have expected your father to give you a name like Joy."

At the mention of her father, Joy stood and walked over to the picture of "Alice drowning in her tears."

"He named me Joy so I wouldn't forget that the world is more than just science and logic—that it's full of mystery and 'jabberwocky'."

"Huh? Doesn't sound like Dr. Newton."

"Oh, no," she corrected him. "He's my *uncle*, my father's brother."

"Where's your father?"

"He's...dead."

"Oh...I'm sorry."

"Died in a plane crash. Years ago. He was a genius...a wonderful man!" Her eyes filled with tears.

To distract her from her painful memories, he said, "Hey, how about that drink you offered me."

"Oh, sorry. What would you like?"

"Well, since I'm in training... How about a Coke?"

"A what?"

"Oh, Jesus!" he muttered, rolling his eyes.

41

Strolling through the dorm, IQ passed the game room and looked in.

Inside, Fig was trying to shuffle a deck of cards and wasn't having much luck. Suddenly, the cards went flying out of his hands every which way!

IQ smiled and walked on.

42

From the silly grin on Joy's face, it was obvious that the pills and alcohol were working. Now that her confession had cleared the air, she was not only relaxed, she was beaming.

Kingman didn't need to be drunk to find her rosy, almost blushing glow irresistible. But knowing that she was technically a "virgin" had dampened his desire to seduce her. He apologized for the way he behaved earlier. "I just want you to know how sorry I am. I had no idea things are the way they are. See, where I come from...or should I say *when* I come from, it's very different."

She sipped her drink and looked at him coquettishly.

"How?" she asked. "How is it different? Where you come from? I mean *when* you come from?" She giggled coyly. "You know what I mean."

"Well, you know...when a man and a woman like each other, they want to get close, real close...they want to...."

She wasn't listening. In her intoxicated state, she was fixated on his sparkling eyes, his strong hands and his moist lips. "I want to!" she suddenly announced.

He was surprised and confused. "Want to *what*?"

She looked at him in a way that made the "what" absolutely clear.

Though this was what he'd wanted, now he wasn't so certain. "Are you sure? I mean... You should be sure! Absolutely sure!"

She swallowed hard, forced herself to look into his eyes and nodded.

"Well," he murmured, "if that's what you *really* want...then I'd be honored."

He stood, pulled her to her feet and lifted her into his arms.

"Where are you taking me?" she asked, her eyes wide, her face flushed.

"To a place you've never been."

That night Joy's circuits were blown.

PART VI

Dire Straits

43

Cheers rocked the NAFA dorms.

Hearing the commotion, Fig stepped outside to see what was going on. His robot dog followed closely behind.

Out on the lawn, some of the Knights were horsing around throwing grapes to each other, high into the air, and catching them in their mouths.

Fig watched puzzled.

Suddenly, TJ tossed a grape to Fig's dog. It didn't react.

"What kind of dog is that?!" TJ wondered aloud.

Other Knights piled on.

"Can he catch a ball?"

"A frisbee?"

"A stick?"

"What the hell *can* he do?!" Smoke finally asked.

Fig froze, overwhelmed by the verbal onslaught.

Hacksaw delivered the knockout punch. "You oughta stuff him and use him as a—"

"It's a goddamn *robot*!" Meathook exclaimed.

IQ intervened. "Hey, you animals! Pick on somebody your own size!"

Scolded, the Knights backed off.

IQ took Fig aside. "How ya doing?"

Fig was still shell-shocked.

"Hey, don't pay any attention to them," IQ reassured Fig, "they're just feeling...homesick, you know." He pointed to the robot dog. "This thing is terrific! Build it yourself?"

"Uhuh," Fig muttered, pulling himself together. "Does everything," he said with pride. "And it's maintenance-free!"

"Don't have to feed it, huh?" IQ acted impressed. "Don't have to take it out for a walk. Doesn't bark when you don't want it to. Don't have to pick up its poop."

Fig nodded, pleased with himself.

"Great! What do you call it?"

"Dog."

"Dog? Just *Dog*?" IQ couldn't resist. "Why don't you get a real dog?"

"What for?" Fig replied. "I've programmed Dog to do everything I want. And anyway, pets aren't allowed."

IQ saw his opening. "What's it like living here?"

Fig was about to respond, but remembered his promise to Joy not to speak with them. "It's okay," he said as he took off with Dog at his heels.

44

The moment Kingman returned to the dorms, he was cornered by some Knights eager to hear his tale of conquest. Furrowing his brow in an exaggerated look of defeat, he confessed, "I...uh don't know how to tell you guys this but...I struck out!"

The Knights groaned in disbelief. As they scattered, Kingman kept up his charade. "Hey, I did my best. I *tried*! I just... I guess she's been hanging around robots too long!" To his relief no one was interested in his excuses.

Kingman was surprised to find Coach Merlin waiting for him in his room. Seeing the troubled expression on his face, Kingman figured he was in trouble. "Guess you caught me, coach."

"Remind me to fine you."

He realized Coach Merlin's upset wasn't about him. "What's up? Something wrong?"

"I've been trying to get hold of game film, records... *anything*!"

"Did you ask Newton?"

"Sure. So far all I've gotten is the run-around!"

"What about Joy?"

"She gave me some graphic animations. You know, x's and o's. *Cartoons*! No real games. Duke, I've got this feeling in my gut that something isn't right."

"Hey coach, the whole damn thing is pretty weird."

Coach Merlin unburdened himself. "Those robots looked pretty good on one play. Do we know how good the new Chinese models really are?"

After last night with Joy, Kingman felt even cockier than usual. "Coach, trust me. We haven't got a thing to worry about. From what I've seen, these robots ain't all they're cracked up to be!"

The Knights' coach wasn't soothed by his star quarterback's swagger.

45

Joy stepped out of the shower, a dreamy look in her eyes. As she applied moisturizer to her body, she savored her encounter with Kingman—every touch, every sensation, every memory. When she finally stood in front of the mirror, combing knots out of her hair, she was brought back to the awful predicament Kingman and the Knights faced. But it felt different now—it was personal.

She dressed quickly so she could get to her computer. Working frantically, she hoped to find something, anything, that could give the Knights an edge. Despite running simulated scenarios that employed dozens of different algorithms, she felt no better than when she started. The more variables she tried, the more she realized the brutal truth of what the Knights faced in the Ultra Bowl. Nothing she did made any difference in the outcome of the game. More importantly, nothing changed the collateral damage—the Knights' body count.

Suddenly, she remembered something Coach Merlin had said about "special equipment." This gave her an idea.

She accessed Dr. Christianson's bionic research. A virtual library appeared around her. She voiced a search term—"football equipment to enhance human performance." A virtual folder appeared in front of her. With a swipe of her hand she opened it and scanned the documents, drawings and mockup designs. "It's a long shot...." she murmured with renewed hope.

46

On the practice field the Knights were busy stretching and warming up. Some of them noticed Fig on the sidelines trying out Dog's new "tricks."

Earlier, Fig had studied old YouTubes of dogs "fetching" and "catching." Using motion analytics software, he had reprogrammed his robot dog.

Testing the upgrade, he tossed a frisbee-like disc into the air. Dog ran after it but jumped at the wrong time completely missing it.

The Knights cracked up laughing.

IQ noticed Fig trying futilely to get Dog to catch and fetch. Seeing the boy's frustration gave him an idea.

After practice IQ knocked on Coach Merlin's door.

"Hiya, coach. Just checkin'—is it true what Newton said?"

"About what?"

"That we can't leave?"

"It's for our own protection," Coach Merlin reassured him. "Till they catch whoever sabotaged—"

"But we can have stuff brought in, right? *Anything* we want?"

"Uhuh...."

"Great!" IQ said as he breezed past him into the room.

A few minutes later, the door to Coach Merlin's room opened and IQ left.

Perplexed, Coach Merlin called after him. "A dog?"

IQ turned and made a sad face. "Coach, I'm soooo lonely!"

As he watched IQ disappear down the hall, a concerned coach shook his head—were his players starting to lose it?

47

Once again Kingman found himself in the middle of a robot football game simulation in Theater C. Unlike the last time, he looked forward to being alone with Joy.

At her console Joy launched another play. The virtual robot teams took up their positions at the line of scrimmage.

Kingman dropped back with a football as if he'd taken the snap. Spotting an open virtual receiver he threw a pass.

The moment he released the football, a 3D light grid beamed across the simulation. The grid, or "net" as Joy called it, instantly calculated the football's trajectory and whether he had completed the pass.

At her console, Joy was totally focused on various screens studying the readings. There was something different in her manner. She didn't coddle or flatter Kingman. She was no longer frustrated, she was desperate.

"No. No! No!!" she cried out. "You're at least five degrees off. Try it again!"

Despite her tone, Kingman kept his cool and ran another pass play.

Again Joy was dismayed by what she saw. "You're not concentrating!" she scolded. "Pay attention! Focus!!"

Kingman muttered under his breath. He didn't understand why she was acting so...differently. He didn't realize that she was trying to save his life!

Inside the simulation, he stepped up to the line of scrimmage once more and executed another pass play.

The readouts on Joy's screen told the terrible truth.

"Ten degrees!" she moaned. "You're off *ten* degrees! What's wrong with you?! You can do better than that, can't you?!" She was almost pleading.

Kingman was bothered more by her coldness than her scolding. With an impish grin, he stepped away from the simulation and walked over to her.

"Maybe," he said in an attempt to flirt, "I need some encouragement."

Busy making adjustments to her programs, she appeared to ignore him.

He bent to nuzzle her neck. "Mmmm. You smell good—"

"We've got work to do," she said, pushing him away. "This is no time for—"

"What the hell's goin' on?!" he demanded. "You having second thoughts about last night?"

She looked away, too full of emotion to speak.

"Look, either tell me what's eating you or I'm outa here!"

She wanted nothing more than to unburden herself, to tell him the truth, but she couldn't. Instead, she got up from her console.

"Okay, I'll tell you," she began. "I can't believe you were voted Most Valuable Player," she said with as much disdain as she could muster. "I've got robots out on the scrap heap that can pass better than you!"

Kingman was taken aback. "Oh yeah."

Turning on his heel, he walked back into the simulation. He'd show her.

Joy sighed, thankful for the momentary reprieve.

48

On the practice field puzzled Knights gathered around Joy.

"This equipment," she began, pointing to the boxes beside her, "will radically improve your performance."

Coach Merlin stepped forward to defend his team. "Why the hell does it need improving?"

Joy was prepared for this kind of resistance. "Every point we win by is crucial—worth zillions to our economy. So why not maximize your performance."

The Knights were on board—"Hey, if the stuff's legal.... Let's see what you've got!"

Joy indicated the shoulder pads worn by a robot player standing nearby. "These can absorb incredible shock," she explained. "I'll need a volunteer."

Reggie held a sledgehammer and waited for instructions.

"Hit those pads as hard as you can," Joy said. "Drive the robot into the ground."

Reggie was more than happy to oblige. "No problem. But this baby must've cost a bundle. I don't want to be responsible for any—"

"Don't worry," she reassured him. "Just do it. As hard as you can!"

Reggie spat on his hands.

Knights yelled encouragement.

Reggie swung the sledgehammer and brought it down hard onto the robot's shoulders. Nothing happened... to the robot. Reggie, on the other hand, dropped the sledgehammer and danced around in excruciating pain.

Joy looked over at the stunned team. "Can I have another volunteer?"

The Knights weren't very eager to step forward. A few began to chant, "Hacksaw! Hacksaw!! We want Hacksaw!!!"

Hacksaw wasn't that keen, either. But it quickly became unanimous and he had no choice.

———————————

The team followed Joy over to one of the hangars that surrounded the field.

Hacksaw stood next to her wearing the special shoulder pads as well as a worried expression on his face.

"Run into that wall!" she ordered.

Confused, Hacksaw stalled. "Wait a minute."

"You're not afraid, are you?" she taunted.

Hacksaw's first run at the wall was tentative. But after he bounced off unhurt, he hurled himself at it with abandon.

Soon other Knights wanted to strap on the "magic pads" so they could try them out. They bounced off the wall, and then each other, as delighted as kids with a new toy.

Fig, who'd been observing from afar, couldn't help but laugh at the comic spectacle.

———————————

Joy held up a pair of running shoes. "They're enhanced," she told the Knights, "to make you run faster and jump higher."

As the team *oohed* and *aahed* over these "jet-shoes," she explained, "Sensors compute muscle changes in your feet and activate accordingly."

The first "trial runs" were catastrophic. It wasn't easy for the Knights to control their "souped-up" performance. Some of them looked pretty damn funny trying to keep up with their flying feet.

IQ, despite his own frustration with the shoes, was glad to see Fig doubled over in laughter, even if it was at his expense.

Gradually everyone got the hang of it. And they were thrilled—these jet-shoes were really something!

Joy handed IQ a pair of gloves. "Think of them as magnetized," she explained. "You'll catch passes you can't even touch!"

It was tricky at first. But when he finally flew through his pass pattern, jumped fifteen feet off the ground and caught a ball that barely grazed his fingertips, IQ was sold.

Even Fig cheered wildly...until he became aware of some Knights watching him. So he stopped and pretended indifference.

49

From her sideline command center, Joy monitored the team's equipment-enhanced performance. Their readings improved significantly and her spirits lifted.

Informed about Joy's equipment request, Newton arrived on the field unannounced to see for himself. Masking his anger with flattery, he praised her. "I see you've been very resourceful."

Joy was excited. And hopeful. "Why didn't we think of it sooner?!" Referring to the metrics on her screens, she announced, "Their performance has improved by a factor of ten!"

Newton hid his displeasure. "Really."

Coach Merlin rushed over. "You should've seen 'em, Newton! If it's legal, I pity those Chinese. Even if they are robots!"

"Wonderful!" Newton declared, forcing a smile.

As Coach Merlin rejoined the team on the field, Newton turned to Joy. "Tell me, dear, will this *improvement* make any difference in the outcome of the game?"

Faced with such a direct question, her bubble burst. "No," she sighed. "Minimal at best."

Newton commiserated. "Too bad."

As he left the field, the hint of a smile dawned on his face.

50

While Joy set the table for dinner, Fig tried to show her a card trick. But he couldn't get it right.

"Shit!" he cursed.

Joy shot him a disapproving look.

"Oh sorry... It's just. I know how to do it. These dumb fingers keep messing it up."

"They're *your* fingers," Joy reminded him. "Just practice—you'll get it."

———————

Over dinner Joy picked at her food.

The awkward silence was getting to Fig, so he tried to cheer her up. "Weren't they a hundred times better? Huh? Especially that catch! Wow, that was something! I bet they're almost as good as robots now! Huh? What do you think? Are they?"

Joy forced a smile but couldn't totally hide her gloom.

51
—

Alone in her lab, Joy was anxious to see how the Knights' improved equipment-enhanced performance played out. She took a deep breath and ran a new simulation of the Knights versus the sabotaged U.S. robot team.

Within seconds, the simulated game was played. Not only were the Knights defeated by a phenomenal score, they sustained catastrophic injuries!

Despite knowing it was an exercise in futility, she played with the numbers and ran one simulation after another in the desperate hope that somehow the result would be different.

52

Fig woke up early the next morning to work on his robot dog. He'd taken it apart and pieces of it were scattered everywhere.

IQ suddenly appeared at the door with a package under his arm.

Seeing the disassembled robot dog, he asked, "What's the problem?"

Fig didn't look up. "I just can't get the trajectory sensors and the hydraulics in sync!"

IQ walked in. "Why don't you take a break."

Fig kept working.

"I've got a surprise for you."

Fig spun around. "For me?"

"Uhuh." IQ held out the package. "For you!"

He slowly unwrapped the bundle to reveal a dog! A real dog. The cutest chocolate lab puppy, not more than a few months old.

Fig was shocked. Flabbergasted!

"H...How'd...did you—?" he stammered.

IQ petted the dog. "There's an exception to every rule, Fig. Sometimes it's called magic!"

The dog excitedly wagged its tail.

Fig stood frozen staring at it. "What's its name?"

"Doesn't have one yet. It's *your* dog. *You* name it."

"Me?" Fig furrowed his brow, then said tentatively, "Dog?"

IQ set the dog on the floor.

"Dog," Fig repeated. "*Dog!*"

The puppy didn't respond.

"Try another name," IQ suggested.

"What kind of name?"

"Any name."

Fig went blank. Meanwhile, the puppy began sniffing around. Fig tried getting its attention. "Chip?...Quantum?... Nano?...." Exasperated by the dog's indifference, he muttered, "I give up!"

"It'll come," IQ reassured him. "You know, I had a dog when I was a kid."

"What'd you call him?" Fig asked.

"Rin Tin Tin."

"That's a stupid name!"

"Then I had another dog and I called him Gonzales."

The puppy began sniffing around Fig's partly-disassembled robot dog. Seeing it, Fig yelled, "Holy Iaccoca!"

The dog froze, then ran over to Fig excitedly wagging its tail.

Amazed, Fig muttered, "Holy Iaccoca!" over and over again.

53

Squinting against the sun's reflection shimmering off the water, Kingman waited by the fountain. With its baroque sculpture of a mermaid lying in the middle of a circular pool, the fountain seemed out of place, more appropriate in Rome than on the manicured grounds of NAFA.

Suddenly, an out-of-breath Joy arrived.

Kingman was hoping she would explain why she'd been acting so cold. "What's up?" he asked. "What's so important?"

She started strolling around the fountain. He joined her. They walked in silence. Finally, she said, "I can't keep lying to you."

He stopped dead in his tracks. "*Lying*? About what?"

"About the Ultra Bowl."

"Oh…" He was taken aback—he thought she wanted to talk about their relationship. "What about it?"

She looked him in the eye. "You haven't got a chance!"

He began to laugh, but the grim expression on her face made him pause. "It's a joke, right?"

"I wish it were."

"What are you saying?! I don't—"

She waved her hand in his face to silence him. "In terms you'll understand…." She referred to a note she'd brought with her, "You've got as much of a chance against these robots as a World War I biplane has in a dogfight against an F-22 Raptor jet." Seeing his confusion, she asked, "You know what an F-22 Raptor is?"

"Sure. But—"

"You *can't* play! It's suicide!"

A cocky smirk spread across his face. "Now there you go again underestimating humans!"

"Ooooh!" she groaned in frustration. She couldn't believe how thick-headed he was. Finally, she yelled in his face, "Don't you hear what I'm saying?!"

He tried to calm her down. "Now, now," he said as he reached out to embrace her, "don't you worry your pretty little—"

She pushed his hand away. "Alright! You need to be hit over the head? Okay. I'm going to show you something."

———

Inside a mist-filled hangar, Kingman braced himself against the cold.

Joy called out some unintelligible commands and machinery started to whir, hydraulics to hum. The mist was sucked up into vents and suddenly he saw them— awesome-looking robot football players, hanging on hooks like slabs of meat in a slaughterhouse. These robots were different, more intimidating than any he'd seen before.

"Those are last year's models," Joy explained. "They're cooled to protect their circuitry."

Kingman shuddered...and not from the cold.

With a few taps of her tablet, Joy activated one of the robot players. It was lowered to the floor and came "alive."

Kingman was stunned. "They look a helluva lot different than the ones we've—"

There was a crashing sound. The robot, at Joy's command, had run right through the wall.

Kingman swallowed hard.

Joy put the robot through an awesome demonstration of speed and power while an open-mouthed Kingman looked on.

"You played against old models," she explained.

"How old?"

"At least 10 years."

"Hmmm," he muttered, trying to recall what Newton had said about the exponential growth of computing power.

"Ten robot years is like a hundred in human years," Joy tried to explain.

He grasped at straws. "We stacked up pretty well against those tin cans, didn't we?"

She shook her head. "Even those 'tin cans' could do a lot more. They were playing at their lowest settings."

"*Why?*" Kingman asked, anger now mixing with confusion and fear.

"To make you *think* you can play against state-of-the-art robots. Like these."

He was stunned, speechless.

"And you can't!" she pleaded.

"But—"

The robot stood poised to throw the football in its upraised hand.

Pained, Joy nevertheless tapped a command into her tablet. "See if you can catch this."

The robot threw a pass to Kingman. In a perfect spiral it traveled almost at the speed of a projectile and knocked him out cold.

Distraught, Joy rushed over and cradled his head in her lap. "I'm sorry. I'm sorry!"

Finally his eyes opened.

"You okay?" she asked.

Kingman moaned weakly, "I don't feel so good."

PART VII

Revolt

54

Sitting in Coach Merlin's room, Kingman gingerly touched his chest. "So you had this feeling in your gut, coach?"

"I knew something was fishy!" Coach Merlin took little satisfaction from having his suspicions confirmed. "How do you know you can *trust* her?"

For a moment, Kingman considered confiding in Coach Merlin about their relationship, but decided not to. "Believe me, I can."

"And the time-travel research?"

Kingman shook his head. "How do you think he got us here?"

"That son of a bitch!" Coach Merlin spat. "He *kidnapped* us!"

"*Time-napped* is more accurate."

"Whatever you call it, we're his prisoners."

"That's right."

"So what's his game?!"

"That's what she's trying to find out."

55

Joy confronted Newton in his office. "According to my simulations, even with the new equipment, they'll be slaughtered! *Murdered!* You *know* that! Why?! What's to be gained? It makes no sense!"

Newton was taken aback by his niece's ferocity. "Your emotions have obviously gotten the better of you," he said in a patronizing tone. "So how can you judge what does or doesn't make sense?"

"But Uncle—!"

"As a scientist, you also know that progress demands sacrifice. And sometimes the good of the many must be weighed against the sacrifice of the few."

She was outraged. "They're not animals you can experiment on! They're human beings!! Their lives can't be—!"

"There's much more at stake than you realize, than you can imagine. We're at a crossroads."

She was shocked by his imperious manner as much as by his words. "If my father were here, he'd never condone this!"

Newton smiled sympathetically and went over to her. "Joy, please," he pleaded, taking both her hands in his. "You're like my own daughter. I know how difficult it's been for you. It's natural you've developed feelings for them, especially for this Kingman fellow."

She pulled away.

Newton's expression hardened, his tone grew icy. "Then I'll appeal to your loyalty. And remind you that during a Stage 3 Alert, NAFA functions like the military. And you have your orders."

Joy looked at her uncle with mounting revulsion, then abruptly walked out, leaving Newton to ponder this new development.

56

Fig threw a stick into the air.

Holy Iaccoca ran across the lawn and caught it.

Wagging its tail, the puppy brought the stick to Fig and dropped it at his feet.

The minute Fig picked up the stick, the dog tried to get it back.

The higher Fig held the stick, the higher the dog jumped.

Fig started to run and the dog chased him.

Suddenly, Fig tripped and fell to the ground.

As he lay there stunned, the dog licked his face.

At first Fig was disgusted at being slobbered over, but soon he was giggling hysterically and rolling around trying to get away, begging Holy Iaccoca to stop tickling him!

57

Lying on her bed, tears streaming down her cheeks, Joy stared at the ceiling trying to figure out what to do. Her conflicting loyalties were tearing her apart.

Unable to contain herself, she scrambled to her feet and rushed into the bathroom to gobble down some pills. Seeing her reflection in the mirror, she froze. She remembered Christianson's warning and flushed the pills down the toilet.

Back and forth she paced in her apartment like a caged animal. Without the calming effect of her pills, she soon boiled over and, in a fit of rage, swept her doll collection from the shelves!

In the silence that followed her outburst, she realized that Fig was standing in the doorway watching her, a frightened look on his face.

Trying to appear calm, she knelt on the floor and began picking up the dolls. "Guess I've outgrown these," she lamely joked, hoping to lighten the mood.

Fig stood frozen.

She needed to distract him. "Uh...How about some milk and chocolate chip cookies?"

He remained silent, but Holy Iaccoca barked approval.

Fig wolfed down the cookies while Joy absent-mindedly petted the dog. Holy Iaccoca's tail wagged happily as Joy soothed herself.

In an attempt to cheer his sister up, Fig wondered aloud, "Why don't you get a FriendBot? They're supposed to make you feel better."

Joy wasn't listening.

Fig shrugged, then popped the last bite of cookie into his mouth. "I wish they could win," he mused. After washing it down with milk, he added, "I know it's impossible! But boy, wouldn't that be *something*!"

Though preoccupied, Joy instinctively reached out to wipe the "milk mustache" from Fig's face.

Finally getting his sister's attention, Fig introduced his dog. "That's Holy Iaccoca."

Although she'd been petting the dog, Joy seemed to see it for the first time. "How do you do?!" she said to the dog, whose tail responded excitedly. "Oh, what a good dog!" she gushed. "Aren't you beautiful!" She shot Fig a questioning look. "Holy Iaccoca?"

"It's a long story."

The dog tried to lick the dried tears from her cheeks.

Joy melted. "What a sweetheart!" She got down on the floor with the dog. "Where'd she come from?"

Fig joined her on the floor. "*He's* a present from IQ."

"What a sweet thing to do." Joy's voice was choked with emotion. Reminded of the Knights, she had to fight back tears. She didn't want Fig to see her cry, so she reached out and hugged him, murmuring resolutely, "Wouldn't that be something!"

58

After Fig left, Joy began thinking about the Blind Awakener's message. She was still conflicted about listening to such subversive rhetoric, especially in her home, so she used goggles to give herself the illusion of privacy. Fasting-forwarding to the last thing he said about the apple and the Fall, she settled back to listen.

"Many among you believe a marriage with our machines is the next step in human evolution. We believe that our vaunted Robotopia is a disembodied hell. Our love affair with technology has diminished our capacity to be fully human. This is the greatest danger humanity has ever faced because, rather than resist, we *love* our oppression.

"The situation is dire. Those of us who resist this de-humanizing robotification of our lives have been called *terrorists* by those in power. But remember, George Washington was called a *terrorist* by the British.

"We are a David fighting the Goliath of an all-powerful Robot Industrial Complex. Yet David defeated Goliath. We call on you, whoever you are, wherever you are, to join us and resist by any means possible."

In an act of defiance, Joy pulled off her goggles. Immediately a virtual screen appeared in the room on which the Blind Awakener's message continued.

"The first step in your resistance is to cure yourself of the insidious Narcissus Syndrome. Having been blind since birth, I was inoculated from the worst de-humanizing effects of this disease. Blindness, in this instance, was a blessing. Let blindness help you see the truth.

"To resist you must first close your eyes against all the reflections which enchant, fascinate and hypnotize you. Close your eyes!"

Joy's eyes closed.

"Now meditate on your breath and blood and your human awareness. Wake up! Wake up from this soulless robotic matrix! Close your eyes and awaken to your humanity."

Joy's eyes remained closed long after the Blind Awakener's message ended.

59

The distinguished TV host introduced his esteemed guest to the global viewing audience. "Dr. Devlin Newton has been hailed as one of the great visionaries of our time. He began his illustrious career as an engineer specializing in robotics and soon became one of the most innovative roboticists in the world. His inventions seemed so far ahead of their time, the media dubbed him the 'Time Traveler' because he seemed to have a knack for seeing into the future. His inventions made him a fortune and the company he co-founded with his brother, General Robotics, became the undisputed leader in the field."

On a virtual screen in the television studio, Newton was seated at his desk in his NAFA office.

"Decades after NAFA was established," the host continued, "it had not fulfilled its mission—an Ultra Bowl victory. To remedy this, Dr. Newton was appointed its new Director. Under his vision and leadership, the United States soon became an Ultra Bowl winner and a leader in robotic technology. I'm pleased to be talking to Director Newton as we countdown to this year's Ultra Bowl."

The host turned to the screen image of Newton. "Welcome, Dr. Newton, Thank you for taking the time out of your busy schedule."

Newton smiled. "I'm happy to be here."

"Let's give our viewers some background. What impact has NAFA had on the U.S. economy?"

Newton welcomed this softball question. "A tremendously positive one I would say. NAFA takes all the new technologies developed by American companies and integrates the very best into new and improved robot football teams. Our efforts over the years have accelerated our technological progress as well as the robotification of our economy which has added significantly to the country's GNP."

"There are some," the host countered, "who feel that the relentless pace of technological progress is not the blessing NAFA claims it to be. What do you say to those who protest that our robotified world is having profoundly negative consequences on our lives?"

"Change is always difficult," Newton replied. "Whenever there's been technological change, there's been accompanying social change. And there's always been a disgruntled few who have warned against it.

"When books were first printed, they bemoaned the loss of memory. When books were digitized, they bemoaned the loss of paper books. And on and on. And yet history moves inexorably forward and we adapt to change. As humans, we embrace change. Do we really want to go back to a time before technology? We'd have to go very far back, perhaps before tools and fire and even language."

Newton assumed a sympathetic tone. "I understand the fear some have of our brave new world. People fear change. They always have. NAFA's mission is to embrace change. We believe we are ushering in a new age in which Americans will have an unparalleled quality of life, liberty and the leisure to pursue happiness."

The host leaned in almost conspiratorially. "One final question, Dr. Newton. Since the point spread in the Ultra Bowl is so crucial to our economy. And every point is worth zillions in market share, how do you maintain secrecy? Surely sophisticated simulations can predict the outcome. And since there is so much at stake, there's certainly a motive."

Anger flashed briefly across Newton's face, but he immediately composed himself. "NAFA's security is our nation's top priority," he replied. "So let me put your mind at ease. As far as simulations, they're just that. They're not reality. Between the simulation and the reality... there's the rub."

Newton sat back in a way that indicated the interview was over.

The host got the message. "Thank you Director Newton for your time. I know all Americans look forward to an Ultra Bowl victory on Sunday."

"All clear," Newton's aide announced, signaling the end of the transmission. "I think that went well."

"Until it didn't," Newton muttered.

"Sir, may I pose a question?"

Newton sighed. "If you must."

"I believe he had a point. Have you considered taking advantage of the situation."

"What do you mean? What situation?"

"The catastrophic economic consequences of the Ultra Bowl. You can mitigate the damage to the economy by betting against—"

"You mean dump U.S. robotics? Unload NAFA's holdings? Bet against us?"

"Yes," the aide replied. "To lose. Yes."

Newton's jaw clenched.

His aide sensed Newton's displeasure. "I'm only doing my job, sir, asking you to consider and weigh various options."

Newton was on his feet. "I'm not interested in *money*!" he declared. "This is not about money. I didn't do what I've done for—!"

"Sir, I—"

"Leave me!"

60

Fig searched the dorms for Holy Iaccoca, asking everyone he ran into if they'd seen his dog.

No one had.

He bumped into IQ but was too embarrassed to say anything.

"How is Holy...uh?" IQ couldn't remember the dog's name.

"Fine. Uh...He's great," Fig lied. "I gotta go," he said and hurried off.

IQ sensed something was wrong, but there was nothing he could do.

61

Joy opened her eyes and looked around her lab.

The Blind Awakener's call to resistance was the spark that ignited in her a determination to revolt against her uncle. She saw how he had distorted her father's work to further his ambitions. Though he claimed he was acting for some greater good, nothing could justify sending the Knights to their certain deaths! And she'd be damned if she'd help him!

Using some of Newton's old memos and his personal encryption codes, she'd doctored his voice and image to create an entirely new and counterfeit memo.

Finished, she'd closed her eyes and gathered her courage.

Now she viewed her handiwork one last time.

Newton, seated behind his desk, spoke with the gravitas of his position as Director of NAFA. "To all R&D department heads. Effective immediately. I am ordering a round-the-clock effort to develop *anything* that will enhance human play against robots. This has the 'Highest Priority' designation and, of course, is Top Secret. All results are to be brought ASAP directly to Chief Systems Specialist Newton and to no one else. I cannot emphasize enough how important your efforts are, and I have every confidence that you will succeed."

Newton's image froze, replaced by the NAFA seal. An authoritative voice warned, "This communication is Top Secret and will self-delete in 10 seconds."

Pleased with her work, Joy closed her eyes once again and murmured a silent prayer before sending the memo under the "top secret protocol."

62

Despite the gathering darkness, Fig frantically searched the NAFA grounds looking for his dog. As he wandered through the complex, sniffling back tears, he began to imagine that something terrible had happened to Holy Iaccoca.

Suddenly, he heard what sounded like whimpering. His imagination had already played tricks on him. So he listened carefully. There it was again!

"Holy Iaccoca?" he called out hopefully.

The whimpering grew louder.

"Holy Iaccoca?! Holy Iaccoca!!"

He followed the sound to some overturned garbage cans in the back of a building. Lifting one up, he discovered the dog buried in garbage. The frightened puppy wagged its tail and licked Fig's face, happy to see him. With tears in his eyes, Fig dropped to his knees and hugged his dog for all he was worth.

63

On her way out of the lab, Joy spotted a security bot. Not wanting to provoke any suspicion, especially after sending the forged memo, she ducked down another corridor to avoid it. She soon found herself in an unfamiliar section of the complex, one she'd never been in before. She quickly realized she was lost. *Curiouser and curiouser* she thought, feeling a bit like Alice after she'd fallen down the rabbit hole. Before she knew it, she was standing in front of a door marked "No Access."

By this time her curiosity had gotten the better of her. "Systems Specialist Newton requesting access," she announced.

"I'm sorry," the security system responded, "Systems Specialist Newton has no clearance."

Joy was mystified—this had never happened before. She'd been trained to follow orders. But she'd already crossed that line by sending the forged memo. "We'll just see about that!" she muttered defiantly and raced back to her lab.

64

"Hey, want some help?" Kingman asked when he found Fig outside the dorm covered in soap trying to wash his dog. It was obvious that the dog wasn't happy and that the kid had never washed one before. Kingman was looking for Joy. Maybe her kid brother would know where she was.

Seeing the Knights' quarterback standing over him, Fig froze.

"Let me give you a hand." Kingman began petting Holy Iaccoca. "I've had lots of practice."

Fig watched in growing amazement as Kingman quickly had Holy Iaccoca enjoying being washed.

"I had a dog, a crazy lab," Kingman said as he soaped and rinsed. "He'd get into all kinds of trouble. But he was real smart. He'd bring me his bowl when he wanted to eat and his leash when he wanted to walk." Kingman began drying Holy Iaccoca with a towel. "And he ate *everything*!"

"Everything?" Fig echoed.

"How about clothes."

"Clothes?"

"Yeah, especially socks and underwear. *After* you'd worn them."

"Ugggh!"

"Try tissues and paper and wires."

"*Wires*?"

"He ate through the wall and—"

"*Walls*?"

"Fences, too. He just had to be free...."

Kingman grew silent. He wrapped Holy Iaccoca in the towel and hugged the dog tightly. For a moment, his eyes watered remembering the life he'd lost.

65

Joy found her way back to the "No Access" door. This time she played a bio-metrically perfect counterfeit of her uncle's voice, similar to the forged memo she'd made earlier, but more accurate than a fingerprint or even a retinal scan. "This is Dr. Devlin Newton, Director of NAFA, requesting access."

She waited anxiously for the security system's analysis.

"Good evening, Dr. Newton," the security system said in welcome as the door slid open.

With a triumphant fist pump, Joy made her unauthorized entrance.

66

Kingman shook off his feelings the way Holy Iaccoca had shaken off the water. Now that the dog was clean, he got down to business. "Seen your sister around?"

Fig stiffened at the question and didn't respond.

Kingman reassured him. "*She* told me."

Fig visibly relaxed.

"She's not in her apartment," Kingman pressed, "and I need to find her."

Fig debated with himself.

"It's important," Kingman coaxed.

Fig's eyes darted around as if looking for an escape route.

"Do you have any idea where she could be?"

Fig remained tight-lipped.

Kingman sighed—he wanted to protect the kid but had no choice. "Look, I know you're probably not supposed to talk to us. But she may be in danger."

Fig's eyes widened. "*Danger*?" He'd made her a promise, but if she was in danger....

"She might be at the lab," he blurted. "That's where she spends most of her time these days when she's not with all of you."

"Where's that?"

"*You* can't get past security."

"Damn!" Kingman muttered.

"But I can," Fig said, a mischievous twinkle in his eye.

67

With mounting dread Joy continued to explore the secret labs she'd discovered. Though violating every security oath she'd ever taken, she felt compelled to get to the bottom of the mystery.

To her surprise, she found not only labs, but rooms built to replicate various official locations. One looked exactly like the Oval Office and another like the Press Room at the White House!

She activated a nearby command console and a virtual screen appeared with a recording of Newton standing in what appeared to be the White House Press Room reading a prepared statement.

"One week ago, the United States was the target of a cyber attack by an, as yet, unknown enemy. The attack was directed at our Ultra Bowl team. I regret to inform you that this heinous act of sabotage destroyed the entire U.S. team! Whoever is responsible broke our security codes, but not our spirit.

"With our economic and national security at stake, NAFA was forced to take drastic action. To use football terminology, with time running out we called a Hail Mary play.

"Using a time-travel technology known as a Chronos Protocol, after *Chronos*, the Greek god of Time, we conscripted—via 'time-extraction'—the best human football team from the past, in the hope that they might be able to replace our sabotaged robot team and compete in the Ultra Bowl."

Newton raised his hands as if to quell what he assumed was the public's outrage.

"I know that for many people, myself included, the idea of humans playing against robots is inconceivable, immoral as well as illegal. However, our national emergency demanded we take extraordinary measures.

"With the authority of the President, the New York Knights football team was drafted into a special ops unit of the United States armed forces. Valiant warriors, these men volunteered to play for their country in the Ultra Bowl.

"We all know how their mission ended. And we grieve their loss. To honor their heroic sacrifice, I urge the President and the Congress to posthumously award every New York Knight our nation's highest honor—the Congressional Medal of Honor."

Aghast, Joy's mind reeled at her uncle's villainy.

68

With Holy Iaccoca at his heels, Fig led Kingman through a maze of corridors towards Joy's lab.

"Officially, I'm not supposed to be here, but Joy taught me how," he said with pride. "In case of an emergency," he added. "This is an *emergency*, isn't it?"

"Yeah," Kingman assured him. Meanwhile, he was lost and needed some assurance. "I...uh...hope you know where you're going."

69

Within its hallowed hall, the Chronos Protocol seemed to pulse and glow like an eternal flame.

Joy, her head bowed, stood before it as if standing at her father's grave.

The moment she came upon it, she recognized her father's dream made real.

Now tears streamed down her face, while a rage began to boil inside her.

Suddenly, a scream erupted from deep within and swept her away on a tidal wave of grief.

70

Joy wasn't in her lab.

A puzzled Fig wondered aloud, "Now what do we do?"

Kingman noticed the puppy sniffing something. The dog started running down a corridor. "Come on!" he called to Fig and ran after it.

Fig followed but had a hard time keeping up.

71

Her mind racing, her emotions in turmoil, blinded by her tears, Joy's grief and anger gave way to despair. She'd hoped to find answers, but everything she saw only provoked more questions.

She thought nothing more could surprise her, until she came upon a sight that took her breath away—row upon row of incredibly life-like robot heads that all looked exactly like the President of the United States!

"Holy Iaccoca!" she muttered as her mind reeled. "What in god's name are they for?"

Spying a nearby console, she tried to gain access to them. She couldn't—their programs were encrypted and unlike anything she was familiar with. Undeterred, she worked feverishly, unaware that a laser security net was moving steadily closer.

72

Holy Iaccoca arrived at the "No Access" door and began to bark.

Kingman paced as he waited for Fig.

When Fig finally arrived he had to catch his breath. Once he'd wiped the sweat out of his eyes, he saw the "No Access" door. "Now what?"

"She's in there!" Kingman said.

"How do you know?"

Kingman pointed to the dog's excitement, "Look at your dog. *He* knows! How do we get in there?"

Fig shrugged.

"Damn, there's got to be a way!" Kingman insisted.

Suddenly, Fig's face lit up. "I have an idea!" He turned and headed back in the direction they'd just come from.

"Where are you going?" Kingman called out after him.

Fig didn't answer. Holy Iaccoca chased after him. Kingman had no choice but to follow.

73

"I knew it!" Joy exclaimed. She'd finally broken the encryption key and hacked her way into the program. "I knew I could do it!"

With a few commands she activated one of the president's heads. It immediately came alive. Its face and mouth moved imperceptibly while its eyes scanned the room. Once they'd located Joy, they fixed upon her.

She shuddered at how incredibly life-like it was and how real its eye contact felt. Realizing she had to act quickly, she gathered her wits. "Okay, let me think," she muttered to herself, "What's it for? How can the president's—?"

"Would you re-phrase the question?" the head suddenly asked in a voice that sounded exactly like the president's.

Her mind raced. "Uh...sure. Uh...Mr. President, I'd like to know...uh...what you have to say about...uh...the Ultra Bowl?"

The president's head looked thoughtful for a moment. Then, as if answering a question at a press conference, it said gravely. "This is not the first time that our nation has been lulled into a false sense of security by our so-called 'friends.' Ultra Bowl Sunday will go down in history as a day of infamy that rivals Pearl Harbor and the terrorist attacks of September 11th 2001!"

Joy was speechless, stunned by the magnitude of Newton's plot.

Alarms sounded. The laser security net had detected an intruder! Joy was targeted. Instinctively, she grabbed the president's head and ran.

She tried retracing her route but quickly found herself apprehended by security bots. She kept running, but they were much faster and closing in. She had only one chance, if she could get there.

With the security bots closing in, she found the room she was looking for and locked herself in.

Out of breath and shaking with terror, she sat at a console and went to work. With trembling hands, she typed in commands that would activate the robot players stored inside their hangars.

She could hear the security bots breaking down the door. She sent her location coordinates and made a run for it.

Too late. The security bots crashed through the door.

Terrified, she dove for cover.

As security bots poured into the room and began searching for the intruder, she cowered in her hiding place.

The security bots were about to find her when, like the cavalry arriving in the nick of time, her robot players smashed through the wall.

From her hiding place, Joy tapped commands on her tablet, orchestrating her robot players as if they were in a game. But now she used their offensive and defensive skills to protect her.

Again and again, just as a security bot broke through and was about to capture her, she directed one of her robot players to tackle, block, or pass an object to disable it. But her robot players were unarmed and eventually, one by one, they were disabled.

Finally, there was only one security bot and one robot player left. As they battled each other, Joy tapped a few final commands, grabbed the president's head and made her escape.

74

In Joy's lab, Kingman watched Fig working Joy's console like a virtuoso.

"What are you doing?" he finally asked.

"I'm accessing her last key strokes. And working backwards."

Kingman petted Holy Iaccoca and anxiously waited.

"So that's how she did it!" Fig finally announced. "Brilliant!"

"What do we do?"

Fig shrugged. "If it worked for her, it might work for us."

75

Joy's escape from the security bots was short-lived. Deadly lasers locked-on and targeted her. Suddenly, she found herself imprisoned inside a light cage whose bars were made of white-hot laser beams. She ran back and forth in the cage from one sizzling beam to another.

There was no way out.

In fact, the cage was getting smaller.

Closing in on her! *Shrinking*!

And when it touched her, she'd fry!

76

Kingman and Fig followed Holy Iaccoca back to the "No Access" door. While Kingman gentled the dog so he wouldn't bark, Fig caught his breath, stared at the door, and muttered to himself, "Uncle Devlin better not find out." He glanced at Kingman as if waiting for a signal.

Kingman silently mouthed the word *Now*.

Fig played Joy's counterfeit voiceprint. "This is Dr. Devlin Newton, Director of NAFA, requesting access."

They held their breath and waited. The few seconds seemed an eternity.

The door finally slid open.

"Good evening, Dr. Newton," the security system welcomed them.

Kingman flashed Fig a big thumbs up. He lifted Holy Iaccoca under one arm and they all entered NAFA's ultra-secret lab. Once inside, Kingman put the dog down and off he went. Kingman ran after him and Fig did his best to keep up.

Holy Iaccoca raced through the maze of corridors with Kingman following close behind until the dog found Joy trapped inside the shrinking laser cage.

"Thank god!" she murmured hearing the dog's barking. Seeing Kingman, she pleaded, "You've got to deactivate those lasers!"

The dog, sniffing too close to the cage, suddenly yelped in pain.

Fig, out-of-breath, finally arrived. Hearing the dog's pitiful whimpers, he rushed to comfort it.

"There's no time for that now!" Kingman yelled. "Toss me those...*things* over there." He pointed to a pile of anonymous robot heads on the other side of the room.

Fig couldn't ignore his dog's pitiful yelps. "But he's hurt!"

"If we don't act fast, your sister's gonna fry like bacon! Now move, dammit!"

Fig rushed over to the pile of robot heads and picked one up, holding it awkwardly in his hand.

Kingman edged as close as he could to the laser projectors while staying within Fig's throwing range. "Okay," he instructed Fig, "now throw 'em to me one at a time."

It was a good twenty-foot toss and Fig froze. "I... I can't!"

"You *can* and you better start right now if you want to see your sister alive! Throw, dammit! *Now!*"

Fig's first toss totally missed Kingman. "I *told* you!"

"It's okay, kid," Kingman said reassuringly, trying to conceal his desperation. "Try it again. You can do it. I know you can. Now come on!"

With Kingman's gentle coaxing, Fig threw one head after another, each time getting closer.

Meanwhile, Joy was transfixed by the searing light bars closing in on her.

At last Fig threw a head Kingman could catch. "That's it! Now you've got it! Just keep 'em coming!"

Kingman reared back and hurled it at the laser projectors fifty-feet away. He missed—the lasers were a moving target.

Fig kept hitting Kingman, but now the quarterback had to find his range. After missing his first few throws, he began knocking the lasers out.

Though the light cage had fewer bars, it grew steadily smaller.

Despite being terrified and out-of-breath, Fig kept tossing heads to Kingman.

As strange as the situation was, it felt familiar to Kingman—the clock running down and the game on the line. But the heads were nearly gone and Fig was nearly spent. Three lasers left, three more heads, three more throws. Kingman had better make them count.

Joy could feel the heat of the light cage as it shrunk around her.

Fig couldn't catch his breath.

Kingman missed!

One laser left. But no heads. Except the one of the president Joy hugged to her chest.

"Give it to me!" Kingman demanded.

"No...We can't destroy the evidence."

"Are you crazy? You'd rather die?"

Suddenly, Fig handed Kingman a piece of lab equipment—a metal thermos. Kingman hurled it, knocking out the last laser.

Free, Joy rushed into Kingman's arms.

"You okay?" he asked tenderly.

She nodded, unable to speak. "I'll be okay," she finally said. Turning to Fig, she reached out to hug him. "You were wonderful!"

Fig pulled away. "You oughta thank Holy Iaccoca." He rushed over to the whimpering dog who was limping badly from his burn.

"Let's get the hell out of here!" Kingman said.

Despite his exhaustion, Fig picked up his injured dog and carried him as Joy led them out.

PART VIII

No Way Out

77

Coach Merlin stared dumbfounded at the president's head in Joy's hands. "He's crazy!"

"Like a fox!" Kingman added.

"It's horrible!" Joy groaned, as the enormity of her uncle's betrayal hit her. "I still can't believe it! Why?!"

Coach Merlin was beginning to understand. "Once he made the switch, he'd be running the show. This maniac wants to rule the world!"

"He's got to be stopped!" Kingman declared.

They were silent.

Kingman called a Hail Mary. "Maybe we can break out. *Escape!*"

Joy shook her head. "Never! NAFA's security is the tightest—"

"There's got to be a way!" Kingman insisted.

Suddenly an idea flickered across Joy's face.

"There is something," she said tentatively. "But it's a long shot."

78

Kingman looked in the mirror as he struggled to knot a formal bowtie. Done, he asked his reflection, "Can you see?" He stepped away from the tuxedo he appeared to be wearing and asked the now headless creature in the tux, "Can you see?"

"Kind of...through this button hole," Joy's muffled voice replied. "That tie better not come undone." Hidden inside the tuxedo, Joy wore a shoulder harness that enabled her to wear a jacket large enough to hide her head.

Kingman mounted the president's head on her headless torso. After he attached it to the harness, he stepped back to get a proper look at the "president" they'd created.

"Sure you want to go through with this?" he asked. "It could get dicey."

"We've already been through that," Joy's muffled voice assured him.

"Alright, let's see what you can do?" Kingman handed her a mini-tablet. With a few taps she activated the president's head.

It came to life, its eyes following Kingman as he moved around the room.

"Damn! You'd fool me!" he declared. Suddenly concerned, he asked, "Can you breathe okay?"

"Would you re-phrase the question," the president's head said.

Kingman frowned. "Maybe we oughta run silent."

Joy agreed. "Simpler the better." She tapped a command into her tablet and pocketed it. "Here goes."

Joy-as-the-president began moving tentatively around the room. She was doing fine...until she stumbled against a chair.

"Damn!" she cursed, "Can't see much out of this button hole."

Kingman took her arm. "Don't worry. You won't be alone."

79

NAFA's main reception building, with its majestic facade and monumental pillars, was a daunting site. Especially tonight. The dramatic lighting for the gala Ultra Bowl eve banquet only accentuated its fortress-like appearance.

Dressed in a tux, Joy-as-the-president was escorted by her "Secret Service" detail—Kingman, Malibu, Reggie and Hacksaw wearing dark suits and sunglasses—up the steps of the main building. Kingman approached the robot guard "manning" the entrance to announce the president's arrival.

"There is no authorization," the guard stated.

Kingman acted outraged. "The President of the United States needs no authorization! Now check those memory banks and pronto!"

The guard scanned Joy-as-the-president. There was a problem.

"The president looks different..."

Kingman held his breath.

"...Taller," the robot guard explained.

All those times calling audibles to counter defenses helped Kingman think fast on his feet.

"Oh, it's those new Italian shoes. You know, with the big heels." He took a step closer to the guard as if to confide in him. "The First Lady made him wear 'em. Thinks that extra inch gives him more authority."

Leaning closer, he whispered under his breath, "You know how wives can be!" From the robot guard's non-reaction, Kingman couldn't help muttering, "Nah, I guess you don't."

The guard stood aside. "The president is welcome."

The Marine Honor Guard snapped to attention. Flanked by his Secret Service detail, Joy-as-the-president entered the grand lobby. A Marine Captain saluted, then did an about face and rushed off to announce the president's arrival.

"Shit!" Kingman cursed, chasing after him. "Captain! The president doesn't want to interrupt the festivities just yet. For the moment, he'd prefer to observe unannounced."

The Marine saluted and resumed his post.

Joy knew her way around the building and led her Secret Service detail to a room adjacent the banquet hall.

"Now comes the hard part," Kingman said as he cracked open the door to the banquet hall and scanned the crowded room. Since Joy could barely see through her buttonhole, Kingman would have to be her eyes.

"My uncle should be up on the dais."

"The what?"

"The main table."

Sure enough, Kingman saw Newton standing in the middle of the "main table" giving a speech.

"I can hear him," Joy said. "If Christianson is here, he'll be sitting with the rest of the NAFA board."

Kingman scanned the faces of esteemed dignitaries until he arrived at the far end of the dais where Christianson was knocking back drinks with a vengeance.

"There's a redhead who's drinking like there's no tomorrow," Kingman reported.

"That's him! Thank god, he's here!"

"Great!" Kingman said. "Now how do we get to him?"

As if on cue, Christianson rose unsteadily from his seat.

"Speaking of the devil!" Kingman said.

Christianson stumbled off the dais.

"What's happening?" Joy asked.

"Looks like he's got to make a pit stop," Kingman replied.

"Huh?"

"*Bathroom.*"

Joy sighed. "Thank god, he drinks!"

Watching Christianson drunkenly weave his way through the banquet hall, Kingman muttered, "Start praying he doesn't pass out!"

80

Kingman guided Joy-as-the-president down the hall. The Secret Service detail followed. He stopped at the door marked "Gentlemen."

"What if someone's in there?" Joy asked, her discomfort clearly audible despite her muffled voice.

"Now's no time for modesty!"

"Would you just go in and check?!" she pleaded.

Seeing she was adamant, he did. A second later his head popped out. He took her by the arm and pulled her inside.

Before she could protest, he led her over to the urinals.

"Hey!" she pulled away.

"And where the hell do you think he's gonna wind up!?"

"I *can't!*"

"Just stand there," he ordered. "Like this."

She tried to mimic his posture at the urinal.

He shook his head. "Like you *mean* it!"

"I... I *can't!*" she insisted and walked away.

Exasperated, he demanded, "Well, dammit, then *where*?!"

Suddenly, there was a knock at the door—the signal from the other Knights.

Kingman pushed Joy into the first stall, then ducked into the adjacent one just as Christianson entered the restroom.

He staggered over to the urinals, unzipped and let loose a mighty sigh of relief.

Meanwhile, Joy-as-the-president peered around the stall and cleared her throat to get his attention.

Christianson looked over his shoulder to see who was there. "Mr. President!!" he gasped, practically pissing all over himself.

———————

The Marine captain jumped to attention and saluted as the "president" and Dr. Christianson were escorted out of the NAFA building by the "Secret Service."

Outside and out of sight of the guards, they propped a woozy Christianson up. He kept muttering incoherently that he couldn't believe the president wanted to speak to him privately on a matter of national importance.

Joy removed the president's head from her tuxedoed body. "Take this to—"

The sight of the president handing him his head was too much for poor Christianson. He passed out!

Everyone looked skeptically at Joy.

"I didn't know anyone else who could be trusted!" she said from inside the tuxedo.

Kingman shook and slapped Christianson, trying to revive him.

"Take it easy!" Joy cautioned. "You'll hurt him!"

As Christianson slowly regained consciousness, Joy unbuttoned her shirt so he could see her face. "Dr. Christianson, please pull yourself together!"

Christianson tried to shake the cobwebs.

"It's me. Joy Newton. You've got to help us." Again she held out the president's head.

Christianson fought through his drunken stupor, trying to understand what seemed like a terrifying hallucination.

"The slaves are revolting!" Joy announced.

A glimmer of recognition appeared in Christianson's bloodshot eyes.

After being briefed, Christianson staggered to his hover-car with the president's head under his arm.

As he flew off, fishtailing through the air, the Knights looked at each other in dismay. "It'll be a miracle," Kingman muttered, "if he makes it in one piece."

81

"We are on the verge of a new day, a new world," Newton declared as he concluded his speech at the banquet. "And I am proud that NAFA has been in the forefront of making this new world possible." Raising his glass, he toasted, "To Victory!"

After a standing ovation from the politicians and industrial power brokers in the audience, he stepped down from the dais. Immediately, his aide approached and whispered in his ear, "Sir, I've just received word that the president made an unannounced appearance at the banquet."

"What?!"

"It hasn't been confirmed."

"Where is he? Why wasn't I informed?"

"Supposedly, he left soon after he arrived."

Newton was perplexed but in front of this illustrious and adoring audience, he masked his concern with a big smile.

82

"So it'd be suicide to play!" TJ exclaimed, summing up the desperate situation they faced.

The Knights had gathered outside their dorm beneath the stars to lessen the possibility of being overheard.

Shock and disbelief written all over their faces, they began arguing themselves.

"What if we refuse to play?"

"Screw that! Let's break out! There's got to be a way outta here!"

"Yeah—let's escape!

"Escape? To where?"

"Yeah, where the hell would we go?"

"That's right—we can't get back to our time."

"We're dead men walking!"

The truth of that statement silenced them. A few Knights began to panic. Others yelled at them to keep it together! It was turning ugly.

Kingman shouted over the uproar. "There's only one way back!"

The Knights quieted to listen to their captain.

"And that's *through* the Ultra Bowl."

A couple of Knights began to protest.

Kingman spoke over them. "This Newton is a ruthless son-of-a-bitch who'll stop at nothing! So if the game doesn't kill us, *he* will!"

Many Knights muttered their agreement.

"I know it looks pretty bad," Kingman continued. "But *suicide*?" He glanced at TJ. "Only if there's nothing you'd fight for. Nothing you'd die for." He looked around at his teammates. "I don't know about anybody else, but

I want a fighting chance." Before anyone could speak, he added, "Joy risked her life to get us some...I guess you'd call 'em *robot busters*. They could make a game of it. If she could lay it all on the line, I sure as hell can."

83

Fig took a break from taking care of Holy Iaccoca's wound to walk the dorm and wish the Knights good luck in tomorrow's Ultra Bowl.

Though the players tried to appear upbeat, it was obvious they were pretty grim about their chances. Fig rooting for them put a smile on their faces.

Fig finally found IQ.

The wide-receiver was happy to see him, too. "How's Holy Iaccoca?"

"Great!" Fig lied. He didn't want to tell IQ about the dog's injury. It would only upset him, and he had enough on his mind with the game tomorrow. There was so much Fig wanted to say to IQ. And he didn't know if he'd have another chance. He tried, but couldn't find the words. "I... uh...hope you...*win* tomorrow."

Seeing a tear roll down Fig's cheek, IQ reached out as if to wipe it away. Instead, he pulled a coin from Fig's ear.

"How'd you do that?!" Fig asked, suddenly smiling.

IQ winked. "I'll show you after the game."

84

Joy shivered but not from the cool night air. Nearby, Fig knelt on the ground. The wind rustling the trees masked his weeping.

Tears welled up in Joy's eyes as she watched her kid brother bury his dog.

When Fig finally stood, Joy walked over, picked up a handful of dirt and threw it on the grave. "Holy Iacocca, you saved my life. I'll be forever grateful. And I'll never forget you."

"You know," Fig said, choking back sobs, "it was a lot harder to train Holy Iaccoca. *Anything* could happen! It was scary at first. Dog did whatever I programmed it to do. But Holy Iaccoca was so…"

"Alive," she said, completing his thought.

"Yeah," he whimpered. "And unpredictable."

Fig burst into tears.

Joy hugged him tightly.

"It's okay to cry," she said, fighting back her own tears. "Life is full of tears. And, you know, tears are very illogical. They come from joy as well as sadness—from loving and from losing things you love."

Wiping away her tears, Joy put an arm around her brother and led him away from the grave. "That's the difference!" she said, her voice cracking with emotion. "Imagine how hard it'd be to program a robot to cry?"

85

Kingman walked Joy back to her apartment. They were both silent, trying to digest all that had happened and all that lay before them.

Suddenly, Joy stopped and turned to Kingman. There were tears in her eyes. "All these years! I didn't understand. My father's death wasn't an *accident*! My uncle *killed* him! He wanted control of my father's research so he could.... God! I *hate* him!!"

Kingman tried to embrace her but she pulled away. "He distorted everything my father worked for! And I *helped* him!"

"Listen to me!" Kingman interrupted. "He was your father's brother, your guardian! You were just a kid! The bastard abused his power and *used* you!"

She fell into his arms weeping uncontrollably. "It's all my fault!"

"It's not your fault," he whispered over and over like a soothing mantra. "It's not your fault."

They stood in front of Joy's door looking at each other in silence. Neither wanted to say goodbye.

Joy forced a smile. Her lower lip began to tremble. Suddenly, she grabbed Kingman's face and kissed him hungrily.

After a passionate moment, he pulled away. "Whoa! Hold on!" he said with a half grin. "I'll...uh need all my strength for tomorrow."

"Don't play!" she pleaded, desperation in her eyes. "Please! I'm begging you!"

Kingman stiffened. "I have to play." He wanted to say more but couldn't find the words. So he took her in his arms and held her tight. "I'd better go," he finally said, pulling away.

Desolate, she watched him disappear into the night.

A few minutes later, a brooding Kingman stood at the fountain staring into the reflecting pool.

"I wanted to tell you... "

He was startled by Joy's sudden presence at his side.

"I'm sorry," she continued.

He turned his gaze back to the pool but kept looking at her reflection in the water.

"I'm sorry," she repeated, looking at his reflection. "I was wrong. Of course, you have to play. And I'll pray that—"

"Pray?" he said with a smirk.

"A peculiarly human trait," she admitted. "Like love." She turned to face him and tried to read his thoughts. All she saw was his pain. "I want to understand," she implored.

He heaved a sigh—he had to unburden himself to someone. Why not her? "When life holds a gun to your head and says choose, you find out what you're made of. Until then, you never really know." He shook his head and shut his eyes. "And then you never forget." He turned to face her. "I thought I knew who I was. Until life showed me I was someone else. Someone I'm not proud of. Someone I'm...I can't live with."

She began to protest and moved to embrace him. He stiffened, took her by the shoulders and looked deeply into her eyes. "Remember me like this!" he said. Then he swept her up into his arms and swung her around until he lost his balance and they fell into the pool...where they finally kissed.

86

A troop of apes foraged in the wild ignoring the presence of the lone human sitting among them. After the NAFA banquet, Newton decompressed by relaxing in another favorite HoloSim.

He watched an ape snap off a branch from a tree, use his teeth to strip it, then shove it into a hole in the ground to fish out termites. Nearby, other apes gathered rocks to crack nuts.

A signal flashed in the HoloSim alerting Newton that his aide had entered. "Yes?" he prompted, his voice weary, clearly not welcoming the interruption.

"As you requested, I can confirm that the president was briefly at the banquet and left soon after he arrived. As to the purpose of his visit? That still remains a mystery."

Newton was too tired to probe further tonight and turned his attention to another group of apes who were signing and waving their hands at each other.

"They seem to be communicating, don't they," Newton remarked to his aide.

"Yes, sir."

Some of the apes were busily grooming each other. There was lots of touching, hugging, even playful tickling that provoked laughter.

"So similar and yet so different," Newton commented.

"Sir?"

"They're so human-like and yet…. What happened? How did we go from this," he pointed to the apes. "To me? To you?"

"According to my database," his aide stated, "about 97 percent of human genes match ape DNA."

"Three percent. That's all it took genetically to make *them* human."

Suddenly, the HoloSim jungle disappeared.

Startled, Newton demanded, "Why did you do that?"

"Sir, I've just received final confirmation about yesterday's security breach at the Chronos lab."

Newton was aghast. "What?! When?! By *who*?"

"Sir, in this case I had to be absolutely certain of who was responsible before alerting you."

"How dare you! I'm *always* to be alerted immediately. There's no excuse for—"

"It's…your niece, Joy Newton."

"*What*?!...*my* Joy?!" he gasped, as if the wind had been knocked out of him."It's...*impossible*! Are you sure?"

"I've accessed *all* the security data—biometric, DNA. There's no doubt."

"Oh god!" Newton sighed, reeling as if losing his balance.

The aide moved quickly to steady him.

Newton pulled away. "Leave me!"

Alone in the empty HoloSim theater, Newton closed his eyes and murmured, "No. No! *No*!!"

87

On the eve of the Ultra Bowl, the Knights were in a very different mood than on the eve of the Super Bowl. Now they seemed more like condemned prisoners awaiting execution, than valiant warriors preparing for a great battle.

There was no horsing around to let off steam. Instead, they isolated in their rooms. A mournful silence permeated the dorms like a black fog.

Instead of practical jokes with paper planes, a few Knights used paper to write letters home to their girlfriends, wives and families, no matter how futile. For some, their "last rites" involved the eating of a favorite meal. And, of course, there were others who prayed.

Walking the empty corridors of the dorm, Coach Merlin sensed his team's gloom. Alone, they were preparing to die, together they might be inspired to live. So he called a team meeting in the gym.

Like his teammates, Kingman isolated in his room. Unlike them, dying was a possibility he almost looked forward to since it would erase the shame that tormented him. As he stared into the bathroom mirror, his life flashed before him. His childhood, his family, his celebrity, the women.... It all seemed like a dream. The man he thought he was had died on the bench during the Super Bowl. The face that stared back at him in the mirror was a ghost. *Tomorrow will be a good day to die!* he thought, as he grabbed the hair clipper and began shaving his head.

A somber team gathered in the gym. Every Knight was there except Kingman. Coach Merlin wasn't sure what to say or how to inspire his men. "The only thing I know," he began, "is that we have no chance as individuals and that our only hope is as a team. We have to come together. As a *we*—that's the only way!"

Suddenly the door of the gym opened and Kingman walked in. With his shaved head he was almost unrecognizable.

Momentarily silenced, the Knights erupted.

Kingman raised his hand for quiet. "I figured it'll be easier to pass as a robot."

The Knights couldn't tell whether he was joking.

Kingman walked over to an empty seat, but before he sat down, he looked at his teammates. "Going into battle, the only way to win is to be prepared to die!"

Like a match igniting a fire, Kingman's words and actions galvanized the Knights.

Malibu walked over to him, ran his hand through his precious hair, and then bent his head as if to be shaved. "Would you do me the honor?"

Soon Knights were shaving other Knights—Smoke's dreadlocks, Reggie's crew cut, IQ's shaggy mane—until there wasn't a hair on anybody's head. Even Coach Merlin's.

"I can barely tell you assholes apart," Hacksaw cracked.

To which Kingman replied, "I guess that makes us a team!"

Boom Boom took the letter he'd written to his family, folded it into a paper plane and let it fly. Everyone joined in what quickly became a paper plane fight until every "letter home" had been drafted into the battle.

Coach Merlin was pleased—the mood had definitely shifted.

Hacksaw appeared with a bag full of ice over his shoulder. He offered to do the "ice dance" if Reggie would do the honors.

Happy to oblige, Reggie poured some ice down Hacksaw's shirt. Everyone hooted and hollered while Hacksaw danced around the cold. Not to be outdone, other members of the Wrecking Crew volunteered. Soon the "ice dance" became a mandatory initiation, as one by one the Knights took turns "icing it up."

By the time the last of the ice was gone, most of the Knights had taken their wet shirts off and were now naked to the waist. Sitting in a circle, heads shaved, chests bared, something primal began to emerge.

Smoke began to beat-box. Using his mouth, lips, tongue and voice, he created rhythms that sounded like they came from a music synthesizer. Following his lead, other Knights began to drum—on the floor, chairs, their bodies, any surface they could get their hands on. The team meeting had become a drum circle.

Coach Merlin stood to speak. The drumming softened so he could be heard.

"When warriors prepare for battle, they go through powerful rituals that help them master their minds. The Cherokee, for example, used special roots that were blessed by the shaman so they contained the magic power of *invulnerability*. The warriors chewed these roots and spit the 'magical' juice into their hands and rubbed it all over their bodies. Why? Because they believed it would shield and protect them, so that enemy arrows would bounce off their bodies like drops of water."

Coach Merlin paused, then added, "They would also dance as a way to embody the powers they'd need. They danced their courage, their strength, their fearlessness. That's how Cherokee warriors prepared themselves for battle."

Coach Merlin sat down and as the drumming grew louder, he wondered, *Would anyone get up to dance?*

Suddenly Kingman stood, but he didn't dance. Instead, he unbuckled his belt and dropped his pants. Then he stepped out of his underwear so that he was completely naked. Only then did he begin to move to the rhythm. Almost immediately, several other Knights stripped off their clothes and joined in the dance. Not everyone could dance at the same time and keep the drumming going. So the men took turns dancing and drumming.

Coach Merlin watched his Knights—naked, their heads shaved—tap into some primal memory and dance like wolves and tigers, eagles and owls, bears and snakes. Amazed, he muttered to himself, "Alone we die, together we live...and maybe even win...."

88

Beneath a star-filled sky, Newton stood on the balcony of his private hilltop compound and surveyed the acres of buildings on the expansive NAFA campus below. Their lights flickered in the clear night air like a small city.

He raised a bottle of vodka to his lips but it was empty. Angry, he tossed it over the railing. The moment it smashed on the ground, he staggered back inside to get more to drink.

Fortified by the new bottle of vodka he was holding, Newton gazed at a photograph of his older brother, Sebastian, and himself when they were young men-on-the-move. Sebastian, the celebrated scientist; he the acclaimed entrepreneur.

He stared at the photo in a kind of delirium and wondered aloud, "Why? Why didn't you see? Why were you so blind?" There was pain in his voice.

He took another swig from his bottle and sat down. Shaking his head in disbelief, he began to laugh. "All you wanted was to visit the past. You thought there was so much to learn there." He rolled his eyes in exasperation as he imitated his brother. *"The past holds the key to all understanding about the present and future. We'll find the answers to all our questions, the solutions to all our riddles, in the past. The past, the past, the past!"*

He collected himself. "Isn't it ironic," he smirked, "that I had to borrow from the past to insure the future?"

He chuckled. "You would've been amused."

He sighed. "You would have been right."

He sniffled, then stifled a sob. "Why wouldn't you allow me to visit the future? Why did you think it was immoral? Oh, I know. You said it often enough. *'It would be cheating, like cheating on an exam, if we knew the answers to our future'."*

He closed his eyes, all the better to remember those heated arguments. "Ideals cannot survive in reality," he mumbled aloud, rehashing those old debates. "That's why they're called 'ideals.' We may aspire to them, but we can't truly live them. That's reality."

He drank thirstily from the bottle, then shook his head. "You were the key *and* the obstacle. I had no choice. Not if I was to fulfill my purpose. Not if I was going to lead humanity to the Promised Land."

He stood up suddenly and almost keeled over. With his free hand he steadied himself against the wall. "Man needs to know the future," he declared to the empty room.

"All great leaders have tried to see into the future. *You* made it possible. But you refused to allow it."

He turned slowly, careful to maintain his precarious balance, and addressed his brother's photo. "You couldn't be allowed to stop progress. No one can."

He staggered over to the sofa and collapsed onto it, sitting in silence as guilt roiled within him. Finally, practically in tears, he whispered, "I'm so sorry. Forgive me. I'm so, so sorry."

Putting the bottle down, he buried his head in his hands and began to weep. Once the dam broke, he was helpless against the current. He'd never allowed himself to feel this pain. Now he was defenseless.

Some time passed before he regained any semblance of control. "And now Joy," he whimpered. "My Joy...why couldn't you just follow orders? Why would you rebel against me? I've loved you like my own daughter. Oh God! Why would you risk...?"

He threw his head back and closed his eyes.

"*Love!*" His eyes flew open. "Damn love! It's the ruin of *everything!*"

89

Alone in her apartment, the enormity of what Joy had done hit her. She'd not only breached NAFA's top-secret security, she'd stolen classified robot technology. She shivered at the thought of what her uncle might do.

Suddenly, there was a loud banging on her front door. She froze—they'd come for her already? Surely they'd wait until after the Ultra Bowl.

The banging grew more insistent.

With nowhere to run and no place to hide, Joy walked slowly to the door, her heart in her throat, as if she were walking to the gallows.

She opened the door and what she saw took her breath away. A sea of shaved heads! And in front, leading the delegation of Knights, stood Kingman.

She swooned.

Kingman caught and cradled her.

When she came to, her first impulse was to kiss him. But she stopped herself. Not in front of his teammates. And not in front of the team she was coaching.

He understood and put her down. "Tonight you'll be safer with us."

"Protected by knights?" she mused. "This is turning into quite a fairy tale."

90

Sprawled unconscious on the couch, Newton was gently awakened by someone.

"I didn't think it would come to this," he muttered drunkenly.

"Come to bed," a woman whispered as she helped him to his feet. "Tomorrow's a big day."

Still half-delirious, he blurted, "I didn't know I'd have to do this."

"Shhh... It's alright," she purred reassuringly. "Everything is going to be alright."

She helped him to the bedroom where he collapsed in a heap on the bed. Lying on his back, his legs dangling over the sides, he let out a pitiful sigh. "How much can one man endure?"

"Can you endure this?" she teased as she stood over him.

Hearing her drop her robe, he knew she was wearing sexy black lace bra and panties, balancing on stiletto heels and striking a seductive pose. Still his eyes remained closed.

"Devlin...Devlin...*Devlin!*" she repeated insistently, trying to get his attention.

He finally opened his eyes.

"Look at what you have to endure," she teased, her hands resting confidently on her hips. She was stunningly beautiful, much younger than him, with jet-black hair, full lips and a perfect figure. She was built just the way he liked, full breasts, small waist, and long legs that seemed to go on forever. In any century, past or future, she was a 10+. Newton usually feasted upon her beauty. But not now.

"What can I do to make you feel better?" she asked coyly in a way that promised pleasure.

He shook his head. "Not tonight."

"Tomorrow is the big game," she said, running her hands seductively up and down her body. "Tomorrow the world will be different. Don't you want to celebrate?" Without waiting for an answer, she dropped to her knees between his legs and began to caress him.

"No," he insisted, his eyes closing. "Leave me alone."

She climbed onto the bed next to him. His breathing deepened as if he was sleeping. She watched him for awhile. "What's bothering you?" she finally asked.

He opened his eyes but just stared at the ceiling.

Ignored, she rolled over to her side of the bed. Now they both stared at the ceiling.

A long moment passed. "Do you love me?" she asked.

An ironic smile flickered across his face. With a weary sigh, he turned on his side and looked at her. "We love our creations."

She rolled over and looked him in the eye. "That doesn't answer my question. Do you love *me*?"

He rolled his eyes impatiently. "We'll talk about this tomorrow."

She was about to protest when he interrupted—"FemBot sleep."

The expression in her eyes suddenly changed as the light in them dimmed.

Though she was staring at him, she no longer saw him. In subtly synchronized movements, she powered down into a sleep position alongside him.

91

On the morning of the Ultra Bowl, a hung-over Newton accompanied by his aide hurried to the NAFA heliport.

"You're absolutely sure it was her?!" Newton demanded. Though he had no doubt, he was going through the motions.

His aide played along. "Her prints are everywhere and security has positively ID'd her. I'm sorry, sir."

Newton grimaced in genuine pain. "She was like my own daughter!"

"She knows too much," the aide reminded him. "The situation must be dealt with."

"What are your recommendations?" Newton asked.

"The game will provide cover."

Newton nodded.

"What would you have me do?" the aide pressed.

After a lengthy pause, Newton said, "What would Socrates do?"

"Sir?"

"I will not order her execution!" Newton declared.

"Sir, I need your instructions."

"Study Socrates—there you will find your instructions."

"Sir..." The aide paused for a moment as it analyzed the writings of Socrates. "Socrates asked questions. As I do..."

Newton climbed aboard the NAFA hovercraft that would take them to the Ultra Bowl. He turned to his aide who had followed him on board. "That's not all Socrates did."

92

The Knights were flown from NAFA to the spectacular Ultra Bowl stadium as "programmers and systems analysts" for the U.S. robot team.

The United States and China were each assigned a section of the stadium complex for their secret labs. A clone of NAFA's labs had been transported and reassembled. The Knights gathered in a part of the U.S. section that had been converted into a locker room.

Before they suited up, a team of MedBots, directed by Joy, administered sub-dermal micro-implants in each player's wrist.

When Coach Merlin asked Joy what they were doing, she explained that the implants would monitor each player's medical condition. Seeing the MedBots administer more rounds of injections, he questioned her about them.

"These drugs," Joy explained, "will enhance their performance, speed healing and reduce pain."

While a part of him instinctively cringed at the idea of his players "juicing"—being shot up with performance enhancing drugs—another part of him was grateful for anything that would help protect his men in their looming battle with the robots.

After their medical prep, Joy showed the team their new uniforms. Made from fabric that looked like metal and metal that had the flexibility of fabric, the red, white and blue uniforms were designed to make the Knights look like state-of-the-art Class-9 robots. To some of the Knights, the uniforms seemed like something a comic book superhero might wear.

"Yo..." one Knight called out, "Iron Man!"

"Football Man, Dude!"

"Ultra Bowl Man!"

"Settle down!" Coach Merlin ordered so Joy could continue.

"The materials are lighter, stronger and more durable than anything you can imagine," she said. "You'll be completely covered. No part of your body can be exposed."

"What about our faces?" IQ asked.

Joy showed them their helmets, whose dark visors completely hid the face, and looked more like something you'd wear on a space walk than in a football game. "Helmets are the key to your disguise," she said. "These visors are one-way. You'll see through them fine but no one can see you."

She activated the helmet and lights in the visor began to flash. "What people see will be the usual glowing lights for eyes that have become a tradition, and the occasional flashing configurations that are meant to give the robots some semblance of expression...the appearance of emotion."

As the Knights filed by to receive their custom-fitted helmets, Joy told them, "These are all hooked up to an encrypted network, so you'll be able to talk to each other. But remember, once you're on the field, you can't take your helmets off! No matter what!"

Before suiting up, the Knights sat in front of their lockers staring into mirrors.

Perhaps they were still adjusting to their newly shaven heads, but as they began their usual pre-game prep—dabbing some anti-glare eye black on their cheeks—something strange happened.

The primal feelings they'd tapped into the previous night resurfaced. Soon the black on their cheeks was joined by other colors, lines and even symbols. Without realizing it, they were applying war paint.

Inspired by each other's designs, they took turns helping one another create elaborate masks. Though their faces would be hidden by helmets and the war paint wouldn't be seen by anyone, it didn't matter. In the greatest game of their lives, if their identities were going to be denied, these masks would be an antidote to their anonymity.

As they added the finishing touches to their war paint, the Knights began to feel as though they were receiving some kind of magic from the markings they applied. Stripes, circles, spirals and triangles, as well as zigzag bolts of lightning, made them feel powerful and protected. Different colors held powers, too. And so the more paint, the more invincible they would become.

Some Knights preferred big splashes of color to symbols, and wound up looking like Mel Gibson's blue-faced Scottish hero, Braveheart. Other Knights preferred the vertical black and white lines that Johnny Depp's Tonto wore.

With the help of the Wrecking Crew, Hacksaw drew painstakingly fine black lines that followed the contours of his face and created the zebra-like mask of a ferocious Maori warrior.

Lance Youngblood chose washes of blue, green and gold to resemble a creature from the movie Avatar.

IQ, a fan of the classic rock band, Kiss, wound up looking like the demon member of the band.

Malibu splashed red and gold paint over his face until he resembled a terrifying tribal warrior from Papua New Guinea.

And Kingman? He covered his face with white paint and then used black shadows to turn himself into a skull.

Dressed in their red, white and blue robot uniforms, wearing their magic shoulder pads, magnetic gloves and jet-shoes, their visored-helmets in their hands, the team gathered for a pre-game meeting.

They were an awesome sight. With their shaved heads and war-painted faces on robot bodies, they seemed like aliens from another planet. Or like a bunch of new superheroes who'd stepped out of a Marvel comic. They looked at each other and were stunned into silence.

A skull-headed Knight stood. As captain, Kingman had to lead. He also had something to get off his chest. "I want you all to know that you're my brothers." His forbidding appearance contrasted with the heartfelt emotion in his voice. "I'll never let you down again. I'm sorry that I did." With his long-festering apology out of the way, he declared, "I swear I will die for you today if I have to. And it will be my honor!"

The Knights were already in a heightened pre-game state. Add to that the drugs they'd been given, the masks they now wore, and hearing their captain's pledge to die for them on the field of battle.

Suddenly the Papua New Guinea warrior named Malibu jumped to his feet. "You all are my brothers," he declared. "And if I have to, I'll die for you today! And it'll be *my* honor!"

The Knights erupted in a *So-be-it!* roar.

A bravehearted, blue-faced Hacksaw stood. "You assholes are my brothers. Some are idiot half-brothers. Some adopted." Knights chuckled at his gallows humor. "And if I have to die for you today, I will...but I'll *kill* you first. And I'll be a happy son-of-a-bitch!"

Another roar.

One by one, each Knight stood and pledged his life to his teammates.

From the corner of the locker room Joy watched in awe—it was the most amazing thing she'd ever witnessed.

When the Knights finished, Coach Merlin stood. He looked strangely out of place without a uniform, without war paint. "I've just witnessed a new Declaration of Independence," he said. "The signers of the original one ended it with a similar vow—'...with a firm reliance on the protection of divine Providence, we mutually pledge to each other our Lives, our Fortunes and our sacred Honor.' Sounds like you've just declared another American Revolution!"

A mighty roar rose up from the Knights.

"All revolutions have to be fought for, bled for, even died for." Coach Merlin paused and closed his eyes for a moment hoping for some inspiration. "I'm not going to give you some speech about what can happen on any given Sunday. This isn't like any football game. It's not even the Super Bowl. It's way, way more than a game.

"This is war. This is a revolution. But even more than all that, this is our only way home. Your bodies may be here, but your hearts are back in the past with those you love, your families...that's home."

Kingman's skull muttered, "We're already dead, this is the only way back to life."

A chorus of war painted-Knights murmured their agreement.

"Duke is right," Coach Merlin said. "Everyone you love is dead, unless we bring them back to life...and the only way to do that is over those robots' dead bodies. Every one of those tin cans is keeping you from being together again with your families, your kids, your life. Every one of those goddamn machines is standing in your way. Is standing between you and everything and everyone you love. And the only way *to* them is *through* them!"

"To them! Through them!"

"We never faced a game like this. No team has. You're the best in the world. And if there's a way to win, you'll find it!" Then he muttered, "I love you all."

Knights nodded and muttered their versions of "love you, Coach."

Kingman stood up and everyone quieted down.

"Something's gone wrong with this world," he said. "Something got screwed up. They're so damned advanced, they've forgotten some basic things. They need to be reminded who they are. Who they once were. And it's up to us! Cause we're the only ones in the world now who can!" Before sitting down, he glanced at Joy.

With their robot uniformed-bodies and war painted-heads, the Knights had seemed to Joy like her sabotaged robots come to life. For a moment, she'd been overcome with grief and guilt. Yet, witnessing these football players from the past pledge their lives to each other reminded her that she, more than anyone else in that room, knew what they were about to face and how terrible it might ultimately be.

Before the Knights stepped onto the field of battle, she had to say something to them. She raised her hand. "Coach, may I?"

Coach Merlin was surprised but nodded. *"You're* the coach," he said, happy to give her the recognition she now deserved. "Of course."

Never having given a locker room speech, she began tentatively, choking back her emotions. But once she gathered steam, there was no stopping her.

"I just wanted to....tell you that you are my heroes. My uncle brought you here to help him put the final nail in humanity's coffin, to show the world that humans can't compete with machines, that technology triumphs once and for all. What he didn't know was what humans are really made of. You've shown me a greatness that the most sophisticated machines will never know."

She glanced briefly at Kingman. "We've fallen under the spell of our technology. Like Narcissus in that Greek myth, we fell in love with our reflection. And we didn't know it. We've willingly enslaved ourselves to the very machines we created. We've become so dependent on them, we believe we can't live without them. And worst of all, we've lost touch with our greatness.

"You've shown me what makes humans great—their heart, their capacity to love and be loved, their willingness to sacrifice themselves for those they love, to risk their lives and die for what they love. No machine, no robot, no matter how indestructible or how intelligent can *risk*. No machine, no robot can achieve such glory."

"No risk, no glory!" some Knights echoed.

"Whatever happens on that field today, you'll be showing the world what it means to be human."

Malibu jumped to his feet. "No Risk, No Glory!"

The Knights picked up the chant and it grew louder and louder. "No Risk, No Glory!! NO RISK, NO GLORY!!! *NO RISK!!! NO GLORY!!!*"

PART IX

Losing Is Not An Option

93

The Ultra Bowl was nothing like the Super Bowl. The only thing the Knights could compare it to was the spectacle of the Olympic opening ceremony. Since the element of human drama was missing, everything was done to heighten the dramatic effect—from theatrical lighting to ground-hugging fog. Even the football glowed!

The robot teams were directed from their respective command centers on opposite sidelines. The Chinese coach sat in the center of what seemed like a battleship bridge directing dozens of systems analysts who monitored the robot players.

Over at the U.S. command center, Joy oversaw dozens of dummy systems analysts, while her command console received real-time updates from the implanted devices monitoring the Knights.

High up in the stadium along the 50-yard line, the red and gold Chinese flag draped the official box of the prime minister. On the opposite side of the field, the U.S. presidential box was festooned with the "stars and stripes." From the adjoining NAFA box, Newton along with anxious board members watched the U.S. team take the field.

The Knights, disguised as red-white-and-blue robots, looked awesome as they ran onto the Ultra Bowl field for the first time. All their pre-game preparation had done its job—they felt invincible.

It didn't last.

The red-and-gold Chinese robots were designed to look like terrifying oriental demons.

"Shit! Just look at 'em!" Reggie gasped, unable to hide the dread in his voice.

As the Chinese robots began their warm up, TJ muttered, "What the hell do they need to warm up for?!"

94

Up in their broadcast booth, a pair of veteran sportscasters covered the pre-game warm-up for their worldwide audience of billions.

"Well, Dan, this is the part the fans love. Each team shows its stuff."

"That's right, Bob," Dan echoed, then added the color. "It's intimidation time, too. Each side tries to psyche the other out."

The robot place kicker kicked the football out of the stadium!

"Bye, bye, baby! Incredible!" Bob yelled, unable to contain his awe.

"According to our instruments," Dan added, "that kick landed over a *mile* away!"

On the field the Knights were becoming rattled.

The robot quarterback passed the glowing football the length of the field right through a target! The crowd went wild!

The Knights were in shock.

Kingman tried to rally them. "Forget it! That's circus stuff—not football! You still need only 10 yards for a 1st down!"

In the announcer's booth, Bob noticed something. "Interesting development, Dan. The U.S. always puts on a show. But this U.S. team is doing nothing of the kind!"

"Could be some new strategy, Bob. Maybe they don't want China to know what they've got up their sleeve."

The crowd began to boo.

"Could be, Dan. But the crowd's not happy about it. I've got a funny feeling that we're gonna be in for lots of surprises."

———————

Both teams lined up for the kickoff. Since China won the coin toss and elected to receive, Boom Boom kicked off.

The Chinese robots swept down the field, plowing through the U.S. defense like an armored tank column and easily ran the kickoff back for a touchdown.

China 7 – USA 0.

Despite their special equipment, the Knights were slow getting up. China kicked off into the U.S. end zone.

The U.S. took their first possession on the 20-yard line.

In the huddle, Kingman looked around at the visors with their blinking lights. It was strange not to see his teammates' faces. "Hey, they're good! Damn good!" he said, trying to rally them. "But they're not *that* good!"

The Knights broke from the huddle and lined up for the first time opposite China's awesome defensive line. Up close to these robots designed to look like blood-thirsty demons from Chinese myth, the Knights swallowed hard.

Kingman took the snap from Reggie and handed off to Malibu on a sweep.

The robot defense swarmed, penetrating the U.S. offensive line like a hot knife going through butter. Malibu was gang tackled so hard, the football squirted out of his hands and rolled out-of-bounds.

In the Knights' huddle everyone was dazed.

Kingman decided to air things out. "Okay. Let's settle down. Give me some breathing room!"

On the next play, Kingman dropped back to pass. The robots rumbled over the Knights' offensive line forcing Kingman's pass.

From out of nowhere the robot safety intercepted the pass and ran the football back for a touchdown.

China 14 - USA 0.

The robots kicked off into the end zone and once again the U.S. offense started from their 20-yard line.

Though they retained possession of the ball, the Knights went nowhere. The robot defense was like a brick wall. In fact, the Knights *lost* yardage on each play! Until finally Kingman was dragged down in the end zone for a safety.

China 16 – USA 0.

Boom Boom kicked off into the end zone.

On China's first play from their own 20-yard line, Hacksaw and the Wrecking Crew didn't know what hit them. The robot offense steamrolled right over them for a touchdown!

China 23 - USA 0.

Up in their booth, the announcers could barely contain themselves.

"What a surprise, Dan!"

"It makes you wonder what's going on in the NAFA box where Director Newton and his brain trust are watching this...*rout*."

In the NAFA box, frantic board members appealed to Newton. He feigned shock and dismay. "I had no idea it would turn out this badly!"

And "bad" wasn't the word for it. No matter what the Knights did offensively, they went nowhere.

Kingman attempted to pass from the protection of the pocket, but the robots' swarming pass rush was relentless! The few times he got the ball away, the pass was overthrown, deflected or intercepted. When he scrambled to buy time, he was dragged down from behind in the backfield.

The running game was even more disastrous. Either the backs ran into a wall at the line of scrimmage or, if they ran wide, they were cut down by a buzz saw of ferocious Chinese linebackers. More often than not, the football was jarred loose by the tremendous impact of the tackle. The one time Malibu slipped past the initial wave of robot tacklers, he was ripped to the ground by the second wave.

The Knights had never experienced anything remotely like it—they were losing more yardage than they'd gained and had yet to complete a 1st down.

Besides being totally dominated, the Knights were being mauled! This wasn't football, this was a bloody massacre!

At her command center, Joy was horrified by the devastation she witnessed on her screens.

On the sidelines, Coach Merlin paced helplessly back and forth as injured Knights were carried off the field on forklift stretchers.

Though the fans were accustomed to malfunctioning robots being replaced, they were shocked by the sight of U.S. players bleeding.

The announcers commented on this new development. "Something we haven't seen before, Dan. Apparently, the U.S. has developed new technology that's so life-like.... I swear it looks just like real blood!"

"Sure adds another dimension to the game! But you gotta wonder—has NAFA hasn't invested too much R&D on this *entertainment* technology at the expense of more practical functions?"

On the sidelines, Fig walked aimlessly among the wounded. Seeing the carnage and hearing the cries of pain, he looked imploringly over at Joy in her command center.

Joy was overwhelmed by the data on her screens that measured the beating the Knights were taking. Not only were they fighting a losing battle with the Chinese robots, if something didn't change, they'd soon be fighting for their lives!

Her mouth cotton dry, she poured herself a glass of water and drank. Suddenly, she began to choke. Finally catching her breath, she stared at the glass in her hand. "Unpredictable," she muttered. "*Unpredictable!*"

Startled by the fireworks signaling the end of the 1st half, she scrambled down from her command center and ran to Coach Merlin. "Coach, I think I've got something!"

95

Up in the booth, the announcers tried to make sense of what had just happened on the field.

"44-0 at halftime!" Bob declared. "I don't know about you, but I'm in shock. How did China do it?"

"Apparently they've achieved a technological breakthrough that's put their robots in a class by themselves. Bob, I think a lot of heads at NAFA are gonna roll!"

"The game's outcome seems a foregone conclusion. The only question at this point, Dan, is how big a blowout will the final victory be?"

"*And* how catastrophic for the American robotics industry?"

"That's right, Dan. What are the consequences for the economy? There's never been—"

"Hold on, Bob. We're getting reports of near chaos in stock markets around the world."

"It may not be a great game, folks, but one thing's for sure—history is being made today! We're entering a new age whose colors are red and gold. A hundred years ago they called China the sleeping dragon. Well, that dragon has just woken up."

"And it's breathing fire!"

Outside the U.S. locker room, Fig was shocked by the signs of blood everywhere. Through the half-open door he could hear terrible screams of agony.

Inside, the locker room resembled a MASH military field hospital as MedBots treated the injured Knights who writhed in pain. Those that were ambulatory slumped shell-shocked in front of their lockers.

A distraught Joy approached Kingman who was getting his ribs taped. "Pretty brutal out there," she said.

He began to laugh at her understatement, then winced in pain. "Anything turn up?" he asked, desperation in his voice.

Before she could reply, Coach Merlin stepped forward. "Okay, listen up! We've taken a hell of a beating.

I'm proud of every one of you. We've still got another half to get through and we think we've seen a flaw in their game."

He motioned for Joy to take over.

"Robots are programmed to play other robots," she began. "So they play the averages; they make the statistically correct move. Everything they do is extremely logical. But humans have one thing going for them, they're *unpredictable!*"

She glanced at Fig who smiled in recognition.

"So our new game plan," Coach Merlin said, "is to start using totally illogical strategy."

As Coach Merlin went to the chalkboard, Joy hurried out.

Though it was her idea, Joy couldn't take any comfort in this new strategy. It was only a band-aid and wouldn't stop the hemorrhaging. With an entire half still to go, the Knights would need a lot more if they were going to survive.

Desolate, she wandered the corridors outside the locker room looking for a place to be alone. She didn't know if she had the stomach to witness the "killing fields" the 2nd half could become.

She leaned against a wall, closed her eyes and prayed for a miracle.

"Excuse me."

Startled, Joy opened her eyes.

A group of men stood in front of her.

For a split second she thought that NAFA security had come for her.

"Are you Systems Specialist Joy Newton?" one of them asked.

She didn't answer.

"We've been sent by Director Newton."

She held her breath.

Sensing her confusion, the man asked, "Do you know who we are?"

His tone wasn't threatening so she scanned their NAFA IDs.

They weren't security, they were *scientists*! R&D!

"Of course," she replied, breathing a sigh of relief, "you're the answer to a prayer."

As Joy and the NAFA scientists hurried back to the U.S. locker room, they briefed her about their top-secret mission on behalf of Director Newton.

Joy pretended ignorance. "Only he would think of something like that. I can't wait to see what you've come up with."

Then she added, "Prepare yourselves for a surprise."

96

When the NAFA scientists entered the U.S. locker room, they were flabbergasted to see human football players. And appalled at their condition.

Joy signaled Coach Merlin who got everyone to "listen up."

She introduced the scientists. "These men have come up with some things that may help. Some uh...*robot busters*."

Kingman and Joy exchanged glances.

Everyone's spirits lifted.

"Sounds of a particular frequency," the first NAFA scientist explained, "can scramble the robots' radar for a split-second so their sensors *see* double and don't know which is the *real* player and which is the *ghost*."

Out on the field, Newton's aide—dressed like one of the U.S. ground crew—approached the U.S. command center.

In the locker room, the NAFA scientist was teaching the "sounds" to Malibu and the backfield. It was a little like choir practice.

"Man, he's gotta be kidding!" Malibu protested.

"Got any better ideas?!" Kingman said.

So they reluctantly learned their parts, doing it mechanically. Until...

"Hey, I know this!" Malibu exclaimed. He sang it, To everyone's surprise, it sounded like an old pop song,

The backfield began singing it the way it was supposed to be sung.

The NAFA scientist checked his instruments. "The readings are perfect!"

———————————

A second NAFA scientist handed out watches to everyone.

"They're set to go off fractions of a second apart to make a continuous sound pulse. That'll create a brief 'hole' in the robots' computation processors—freezing them— which should give you a chance to—"

"Knock 'em on their asses!" Hacksaw shouted.

———————————

At the U.S. command center, Newton's aide refilled the water in Joy's pitcher.

———————————

In the locker room, a third NAFA scientist strapped on a strange-looking belt. "These buckles are powerful magnets," he explained. "Twisting the buckle, like this, shifts the magnetic field. It'll distort the robots' tracking sensors and throw their targeting accuracy off by several degrees, giving you a few extra inches to—"

The signal for the 2nd half sounded. The Knights dragged themselves to their feet and began filing out.

The fourth and last NAFA scientist approached Joy and handed her a box. "I've dusted off some of the old stealth technology. There's just one problem...."

97

As halftime came to an end, Newton joined the president in his box.

"We had no idea it would be this bad, Mr. President. On behalf of NAFA, I apologize for this catastrophe."

The president ignored him, his attention focused on the teams retaking the field for the 2nd half.

The Knights' offense couldn't wait to try out their "robot busters." On the line of scrimmage for their first offensive play, they sang the "golden oldie," hesitantly at first and then with more gusto. But bodies began to sway, heads bobbed and even fingers snapped.

Whistles! Penalty flags!

On the sidelines, Coach Merlin threw his hat on the ground.

Joy looked over at the NAFA scientist who shrugged helplessly.

In the huddle Kingman was pissed. "Lose the goddamn stage show!"

The Knights' offense lined up opposite the robots. 2nd down. Again they sang, but this time nobody moved. The ball was snapped. And something strange happened....

The robot defense hesitated, doing double-takes as if seeing extra players opposite them. When they finally rushed, it was too late—the Knights' blockers had the angle and momentum, and were pushing them back!

Malibu took the handoff from Kingman and plunged through the line. For the first time robot linebackers missed their tackles! Malibu picked up a 1st down!

The announcers could barely contain their excitement. "Looks like NAFA made some adjustments at halftime, Dan."

"Sure seems that way, Bob. But I'm afraid it's a case of too little too late."

In the huddle Kingman was pumped. "Way to go! If this other stuff is as good, hell, we might make a game of it! Okay, set your watches."

They lined up against China's robot defense.

On the watches' alarm the ball was snapped. The synchronized sound pulse momentarily froze the robots! The Knights got the jump and knocked them on their titanium asses, opening another big hole through which Malibu dove for a 7-yard gain.

In the huddle the Knights were high-fiving.

"Let's try it again," Kingman called. "With a delay."

This time Kingman took the snap and rolled out. IQ came around from his wide receiver position and took the handoff from Kingman. It was a reverse. Blockers were out in front of IQ leading the way. The robot pursuit was relentless and about to steam-roll right over IQ. Suddenly, the synchronized pulse of the watch alarms went off!

The robots froze as if their plugs had been pulled! Only for a split-second. By the time they were back online, it was too late. U.S. blockers were plowing them out of IQ's way for a 14-yard pickup and another 1st down.

At China's command center, systems analysts frantically checked their screens, trying to diagnose the anomalies that were afflicting their robots.

In the huddle, Kingman called another play. "Let's give these belts a shakedown run. Pitchout left. Turn your buckles hard right 90 degrees."

Everyone adjusted their belt buckles.

"Let's rock n' roll!" Malibu crowed.

The ball was snapped. Kingman rolled out to his left and pitched out to Malibu, but the robot blitz had broken through the offensive line into the backfield and was about to wrap Malibu up for a big loss.

Then, lo and behold, confounded by the distorted magnetic field, one robot after another missed the tackle as Malibu feinted, spun and danced for another 1st down.

The U.S. fans went wild.

In the huddle Kingman sensed the tide turning. "If we put it all together, we'll put some points on the board."

As one, the Knights chorused, "Rock n' roll!!!"

In an incredible series of plays, the Knights combined the singing, the watch alarm, and the magnetic belts. And it *worked*!

The crowd roared as the U.S. mounted their first sustained drive.

Meanwhile, China's command center was totally baffled by what they were seeing on their screens.

From the robots' point of view, the U.S. team appeared to momentarily double; or the data stream froze; or their screens just went blank!

Frantically, they tried to compensate.

To no avail—with the aid of their "robot busters," the U.S. finally scored a touchdown.

The Knights were so elated you'd think they'd won.

China 44 - USA 7.

In the NAFA box there was jubilation.

Newton, deluged by congratulations, masked his irritation with a big smile.

98

The Wrecking Crew took the field. Hacksaw's confidence had returned. Feeling a bit like his old self, he rode the demonic-looking robot opposite him. "You ugly hunk of tin! I'm gonna rip your circuits apart! You poor excuse for a food processor! Get ready for junkyard heaven!"

When the ball was snapped, the robot seemed pre-occupied. Hacksaw knocked it on its ass and made the tackle!

On the next play, Hacksaw tried trash-talking again. "I'm gonna kick your tin butt! You oil guzzling, metal-bellied, shit-faced, asshole! When I'm through with you, your momma won't recognize you! You miserable son-of-a—!"

Once again the robot was momentarily discombobulated, so Hacksaw could plow into it and break up the play. Certain he'd stumbled onto something, he called "time out."

From her command center, Joy listened in as Hacksaw excitedly reported to Coach Merlin on the sidelines.

"Are you nuts?!" Coach Merlin responded. "Those things don't understand what you're saying!"

Joy interrupted. "Sure they do! We've had language capabilities for years. It's built into all systems. He's right. *Insult* them! They haven't been programmed to deal with something as complex as insults! It'll totally confuse them!"

Hacksaw ran back to the huddle and relayed the new tactic to the Wrecking Crew. As they lined up on defense, the Knights bombarded the robot offense with a litany of insults. The robots seemed stunned by the abuse! It was just the edge the Wrecking Crew needed to crash through China's offensive line and sack the robot quarterback for a big loss.

China had to kick.

Employing the "robot-busters" and the newly discovered "insult" tactic, the U.S. mounted a remarkable comeback. With a few key plays—an electrifying run by Malibu and an interception by Smoke—the Knights put another 14 points on the scoreboard.

China 44 - USA 21.

Despite the rapturous mood of everyone else in the NAFA box, Newton grew increasingly troubled.

Down on the sidelines, the Chinese command center worked feverishly to correct the new malfunctions.

The Knights' momentum slowed and finally ground to a halt.

Boom Boom kicked a field goal.

China 44 - USA 24.

China's offense returned to its earlier form—all systems go—and again ran roughshod over the U.S. defense. Despite the Wrecking Crew's verbal abuse, the Chinese robots marched easily down the field until they were threatening inside the U.S. 20-yard line.

At the U.S. command center, Joy frantically tried to find some other weakness in the robots' game. She ran a simulation and poured herself a drink of water from the pitcher. When her screens displayed the results, her eyes lit up. She radioed Coach Merlin—"Jokes!"

"What?"

"Tell them jokes!"

"Are you joking?"

"I'm dead serious."

With a shrug, the Knights coach signaled for a "time out."

———

Hacksaw listened skeptically as his coach relayed Joy's instructions. "You gotta be kidding?!"

Coach Merlin shrugged and pointed to Joy.

"Shit, I can't think of any jokes," Hacksaw grumbled.

Kingman, who'd been listening, yelled, "Where's Reggie? Someone get Reggie!"

Reggie ran over.

Hacksaw grabbed him, "Tell me a joke!"

Reggie was stunned—he couldn't believe that the Knight who ragged him the most about his jokes wanted to hear one. "You really want me to—"

Kingman broke in. "Reggie, make like a comic!"

From Joy's vantage point at the command center, it didn't sound too promising. Though their faces were hidden, she could hear Reggie laughing as he told a couple of jokes. But Hacksaw, Coach Merlin and Kingman listened in stony silence.

Hacksaw ran back onto the field and relayed the new play. The Wrecking Crew thought he was nuts, but they'd try anything.

As the Knights' defense lined up nose to nose with the terrifying Chinese robots, they told them Reggie's jokes.

"A guy goes into a bar...."

"A rabbi and a priest are in heaven...."

"This farmer's got 3 daughters...."

The robots didn't exactly laugh, but when the ball was snapped, they seemed perplexed...long enough for the Wrecking Crew to get the jump, crash through their line, penetrate into the backfield and gang tackle the big robot running back for a loss.

While the Wrecking Crew butted heads in celebration, Hacksaw looked to the sidelines and gave Reggie the thumbs up.

China called "time-out." There was frantic activity at their command center as they checked, re-checked and made adjustments.

On the U.S. sidelines, Reggie did his standup routine, basking in everyone's undivided attention.

On the next play, the trash-talking, joke-telling Wrecking Crew recovered a fumble! Knights took possession.

100

Kingman was about to lead the offense onto the field when Joy radioed in.

"Coach, talk to them in paradoxes."

"What?"

"*Paradoxes!*"

"*What*?!"

"You know what they are, don't you?"

He shrugged.

"Paradoxes are illogical," she explained. "It'll have them chasing their own tail."

Kingman shrugged—he didn't get it either.

In the huddle, the Knights looked at Kingman like he was nuts! "Para... *what*?!" they parroted.

"I don't know!" Kingman confessed.

IQ explained. "A paradox is a statement that contradicts itself. It's also called an *oxymoron*."

"You sound like a fuckin' moron!" Malibu scowled.

Kingman took the reins. "Get to the point!"

IQ tried. *"I have nothing to say and I'm saying it."*

They looked at him strangely.

IQ tried again. "Or...uh...*Nostalgia ain't what it used to be!*" Seeing their confusion, he explained, "It cancels itself out! Try this—*Everything I say is a lie!*"

In frustration, Reggie declared, "I'm stickin' to jokes!"

With time running out, Kingman broke the huddle. "Showtime!"

As they lined up on offense, the Knights announced, "Everything I say is a lie!" before either insulting the robot opposite or telling it a joke.

The play—a draw up the middle—was executed like clockwork for a big gain!

101

At the U.S. command center Joy was feeling dizzy. As her perceptions became increasingly distorted, she had difficulty monitoring her screens. She took another drink of water from the pitcher to quench her growing thirst. Meanwhile, the box of "stealth uniforms" lay nearby, apparently forgotten.

Using the paradox tactic. Kingman threw a play-action pass to IQ for a touchdown.

China 44 - USA 31.

Hacksaw and the Wrecking Crew held.

Up in the broadcast booth, the announcers excitedly commented on the game.

"This isn't the same U.S. team we saw in the 1st half, Bob. Not only are they making a game of it, but this new technology of theirs is really something else."

"I have to agree with you, Dan. It's so effective, there's a wild rumor going around that the U.S. team *aren't* robots! It's that incredible new technology NAFA's built into this new model. I'll admit I was critical of it at first, but it sure adds a whole new dimension to the game. Can you imagine it, Dan, the idea of humans playing against robots?! Unbelievable!"

As the U.S. moved the ball down the field, the announcers continued their upbeat commentary. "The tide's definitely turned, Dan. The U.S. seems to have gotten China's number. And the Chinese seem to be in disarray."

"I'll tell ya, Bob, if robots had anything like morale, I'd say they've lost theirs."

At China's command center, frantic systems analysts tried to correct the strange malfunctions disabling their robots.

Over at the U.S. command center, Joy stared blankly at the pitcher of water. Something clicked!

"Water!" she gasped. "It's the *water!!*"

To celebrate, she poured herself another glass from the pitcher.

"And shweat! And tearsh!!" she mumbled as if drunk.

The robots' sensitive circuitry was defenseless against the dissolving liquids humans exude—their blood, sweat and tears.

Pleased with her detective work, she took another drink. And began hallucinating—things seemed to disappear!

Suddenly, she remembered the "stealth" uniforms!

She needed to alert Coach Merlin, but forgot that she could simply radio him.

Instead, she began to climb down from the command center. Though she'd done it thousands of times before, in her drugged state it was like climbing down a mountain.

On the field, China called another "time-out."

Kingman hurried to the sidelines to confer with Coach Merlin.

At last Joy made it to the ground and headed in Coach Merlin's direction, weaving and stumbling as if drunk.

When she began walking in circles, bewildered and concerned Knights gathered around her.

Seeing Joy's distress, Kingman rushed to her side.

"What is it? What's wrong?!"

"Water!" she announced drunkenly. "It's the *water*!"

"Huh?" Kingman was stumped.

Her speech was so thick and slurred, she was barely intelligible. "Ditholving their thircuits!"

King was concerned. "We gotta get you to a doctor!"

She waved him off. "The uniforms." She pointed— "In the box."

Kingman nodded. "Okay. Save your strength."

She had one more thing to say. "One problem." She keeled over.

Kingman caught her, picked her up and carried her to the stretcher crew.

A hundred thousand screaming fans suddenly went dead quiet seeing the drama that was unfolding on the U.S. sideline.

Joy fought to remain conscious. She willed herself to speak. In barely a whisper she said, "Massive energy requirements. Only one player at a time. And only once."

Certain Newton was responsible for Joy's condition, Kingman glared up at the NAFA box.

102

If Newton, watching from his box, was shaken by seeing Joy lifted onto a stretcher, he was shocked by what happened next.

Kingman suddenly took off his visored-helmet to kiss Joy before she was taken away.

The crowd gasped.

Fig, accompanying Joy's stretcher, yelled to Kingman—"You can do it! I know you can!"

The crowd was in an uproar—*If it wasn't a robot, what was that skull-headed creature?*

Coach Merlin shouted, "Get your damn helmet back on!"

Kingman watched Joy being wheeled away, then suddenly realized that all eyes were on him. He looked around the hushed stadium at the stunned crowd. Something in him rebelled. "To hell with this charade!"

An eerie hush fell over the crowd as Kingman began rooting around in an old duffle bag on the U.S. sideline. Finally, he found what he was looking for—his New York Knights helmet—and he strapped it on.

The crowd began to buzz with excitement.

That's all Malibu needed—he yanked off his visored-helmet, too, revealing his war painted-face.

"Man, I've been wanting to do this all goddamn day!" he declared as he ran to the sideline.

What were they? the flabbergasted crowd wondered, *Aliens from another planet?* A hundred thousand people held their collective breath.

Seeing a helmet-less Malibu approach, Kingman tossed him his old helmet.

Immediately, the rest of the Knights followed suit.

Watching the U.S. team strap on their New York Knights helmets, the crowd gasped—*They're HUMANS!*

Pandemonium rocked Ultra Bowl stadium.

Up in their booth, the announcers were on their feet.

"They're *humans*! It's true! The U. S. team is human! This is unbelievable! It's *impossible*! Dan, help me out here!"

"I'm as shocked as you are, Bob. As we all are! Listen to the crowd! Holy Iaccoca!"

103

Inside the NAFA box there was hand-wringing and hair-pulling. Board members looked around for Newton, but he wasn't there.

He had returned to the presidential box to do damage control. "You ordered me to do whatever I could to mitigate the disaster," he reminded the president. "The lesser of two evils...."

In broad brushstrokes, Newton quickly de-briefed him on the Chronos Protocol. To his surprise, the president just listened. Relieved, Newton added, "Discovery was always a possibility, Mr. President. Once again we're confronted with the undeniable fact that humans, unlike robots, are extremely unreliable. But let me assure you, I've taken this contingency into account."

The president remained grim and made no reply.

Now that their secret had been revealed, there was an added poignancy to the Knights' epic struggle. They paid dearly for every inch, every yard, every 1st down. Their impossible battle against these awesome football-playing machines assumed mythic dimensions, touching deep chords within everyone who witnessed it. The blood was real and the agony was felt by all. There wasn't a dry eye in the world.

In the stadium and around the globe, spectators were on the edge of their seats caught up in the life and death drama being played out in the Ultra Bowl. Despite the insurmountable odds against them, despite the terrible injuries they sustained, with the help of their own blood, sweat and tears, the human U.S. team staged a miraculous comeback.

The disciplined NAFA technocrats, many in tears, cheered themselves hoarse.

At their command center, the Chinese systems analysts couldn't conceal their admiration.

Even the Chinese fans found themselves rooting for the "Humans!"

A dazzling run by Malibu. A pass from Kingman to IQ. The U.S. was on the move.

Up in their booth the announcers were beside themselves.

"I can't believe it! No way can humans play against robots! It's *impossible*! It's.... And yet they're making a game of it, Dan! If I didn't see it with my own eyes...."

"*Who* are they?! Where'd they come from?! How the hell are they doin' it?!"

104

In the presidential box, Newton watched everyone, including the president, yell themselves hoarse. It was increasingly difficult for him to conceal his rage behind the facade of fanatic fandom.

The Knights scored again.

China 44 – USA 38.

Newton had never imagined these humans making a game of it, let alone the possibility of them winning! Inconceivable! Yet it was happening. Unless he acted quickly, all his hopes for the future, all his dreams for a more perfect union, would be lost forever. All he'd done, all he'd sacrificed, would have been for nothing. His mind raced with options. And they all pointed to one drastic course of action. A last resort.

While the presidential box was caught up in the hysteria sweeping the stadium, Newton moved closer to the president and whispered in his ear. "Very moving, isn't it. I must admit it's quite a surprise."

The president ignored him and continued cheering the team on.

"Mr. President," Newton said loudly so he could be heard above the cheering, "wouldn't you like to go down to the field to meet the players?" Hidden in his hand, he held a small laser weapon that he jabbed into the president's back. "I can take you down onto the field right now," Newton said with a big smile as he guided the president passed his cheering staff and out of the presidential box. To his relief, the Secret Service detail was so caught up in the frenzy, they didn't seem to notice the president leaving.

105

The 4th quarter wound down and the Wrecking Crew's defense held. China had to kick and the Knights took possession for the last time deep in their own territory.

A thunderous chant rocked the stadium, *"Go Humans Go!"*

Time was running out—1:42...:41...:40....

On the sidelines, Kingman checked with Coach Merlin. "Any word about Joy?"

Coach Merlin shook his head.

Kingman looked over at the now vacant command center and suddenly remembered. "Hey, what about those...stealth uniforms? Let's give 'em a try!"

The announcers couldn't understand why the Knights would risk a penalty just so IQ and Malibu could put on new uniforms.

"This is very strange, Dan! Why is the U.S. changing uniforms now? It's taking too much time. It's—!"

Whistles blew—"delay of game."

The crowd booed.

After the penalty, Malibu lined up as a flanker outside the tight end.

Kingman took the snap and rolled out to the sidelines in Malibu's direction. Malibu was running towards him and suddenly disappeared!

Fighting every football instinct he had, Kingman counted to three, then handed the ball off to thin air! He held his breath until he glimpsed it floating past him tucked away in the arms of an "invisible" Malibu Malone.

Incredibly, the robot pursuit couldn't see Malibu! Meanwhile, the football magically floated to the sidelines as the now invisible running back streaked for the corner.

The one thing Joy hadn't warned them about was that the stealth mode lasted only a few seconds. So just as Malibu was about to break free into the open field, he *reappeared*!

Reggie, who was out in front blocking, didn't see Malibu until it was too late and knocked him over!

On the sidelines Coach Merlin threw a fit.

The clock was running down—:52...:51 seconds.

IQ rushed over to Kingman. "Duke, I can beat their safety!"

Kingman called another "time-out."

106

Kingman conferred with Coach Merlin. Youngblood, his uniform spotless, listened in.

"I don't think you'll have enough time!" Coach Merlin said.

"Coach," Youngblood interrupted. "Let me scramble for time, then I'll lateral."

Kingman jumped in. "Then you'll be—"

"The decoy!" Youngblood insisted.

"You're gonna get *killed!*" Kingman countered.

"But *you'll* have enough time—"

"To throw up a prayer," Kingman conceded.

Youngblood was resolute. "It's *my* funeral."

Coach Merlin stepped in. "You sure you want to do this?"

"I've had it pretty easy so far," Youngblood replied. "Time to see what the future is really like."

The Knights lined up in a shotgun formation with Youngblood in the backfield. The ball was snapped to him and he began to scramble from the blitzing Chinese robots that were in hot ten-ton pursuit.

On the sidelines, Coach Merlin yelled, "Lateral! Damn it, *lateral!!*"

But Youngblood, who hadn't played until now, was fresh and kept scrambling to gain time.

Meanwhile, IQ ran his pass pattern downfield, but the robot safety locked onto him and wouldn't bite on any of his fakes.

Just as Youngblood was about to be flattened by the robot pass rush, he tossed the football across the field to Kingman. And then...it was as if Youngblood had been run over by a Mack truck!

Kingman caught the football and set himself to throw. He didn't have much time before the changing tide of the robot pursuit cut him down.

Downfield, IQ couldn't shake the robot safety. So he activated the "stealth" mode and *disappeared*.

The robot safety did a double take. Totally confounded, it moved first in one direction, then in another as if having an epileptic fit, all the while scanning its sensors for some sign of the receiver. It found nothing!

Kingman waited until the last possible second. The robot pass rush bore down on him. Just as he was about to be steam-rolled into the ground, he reared back and threw....

It was a high arcing spiral.

The robot safety instantly honed in on it and headed for a rendezvous.

Suddenly, IQ *reappeared* a few steps ahead. He had the robot beat, but the race was on. Despite his jet-shoes, the robot was gaining on him.

The ball was slightly overthrown. IQ hoped that his "magic" hands and those magnetic gloves could do the rest. He leapt into the air with the robot safety blanketing him.

The crowd held its breath.

The ball sailed past IQ's outstretched fingers, but he managed to tip it into the air and then juggled it on his way down. When he finally crashed to the ground, he'd made an extraordinary flying, fingertip catch right near the goal line!

Kingman got slowly to his feet. Though dazed, he heard the crowd's roar and smiled. 1st and goal!

The Knights' celebration was short-lived when they saw Youngblood lying motionless where he'd been gang-tackled. Unconscious and about to be carried off the field by a forklift, his teammates ran over from the sidelines to bear him off like an honor guard.

107

"I have another surprise for you, Mr. President, if you'll please..."

Instead of taking the president down to the playing field, Newton led him at gunpoint to NAFA's secret labs within the U.S. section of Ultra Bowl stadium.

"They'll never even miss you!" Newton taunted. "They'll think we went to stretch our legs!"

Arriving at the entrance to the secret lab, Newton announced, "Dr. Devlin Newton requesting access." As he waited for security to confirm his biometrics, he gloated, "I've paid a high price, Mr. President, a very high price.

To achieve greatness, one can't shrink from whatever means are necessary."

The pneumatic hiss of the door opening was followed by the security system's welcome.

Newton prodded the president in the back with his laser. "After you, Mr. President."

108

On the sideline Kingman finished conferring with Coach Merlin. He started back onto the field, then stopped. "Got any more tricks up your sleeve, Coach?"

"We've used up every trick in the book and then some." After a moment's pause, Coach Merlin added, "How about a prayer?"

"We already did a Hail Mary."

"I mean a real one."

In the huddle, Kingman called the play.

"Okay. Back to basics. Power Draw. Malibu, you're goin' over the top." He let it sink in. "There's no other way. Not if we want to win. And we didn't come this far to lose!" Now that they were wearing their own helmets, he looked everybody in the eye. "We all know how much this is gonna cost. And who's gonna pay the most."

Everyone cast a questioning look at Malibu.

"No risk, no glory!" he answered resolutely.

"Let's have a moment of silence," Kingman said. "For everyone who's helped us come this far." Then he added, "Let's kick ass!"

The Knights shouted, "Amen!"

They broke from the huddle and were confronted by China's awesome "goal line" defense. As they lined up—humans versus robots—the world held its breath.

The Knights' blood, sweat and tears had paved the way. So this time there were no "robot busters"—no singing, no insults and no jokes. No watches. No paradoxes. And no magnetic belts. Just good, old-fashioned 21st century football.

Kingman called off the count. The ball was snapped. The clock ticked off the last few seconds as time seemed to slow and the Knights gave it everything they had!

On the line of scrimmage it was a fight to the death—skin tore, blood flowed, bones splintered, ribs cracked and the air exploded with terrible groans of effort and cries of pain as proud humans battled merciless machines.

Kingman handed off to Malibu. They locked eyes as if saying "goodbye."

Malibu took the football and accelerated, straining every muscle to reach maximum speed, then launched himself into the air....

On the goal line it was mayhem as the Knights' offensive line tried to fend off the robot linebackers who were on a collision course with Malibu. It was a mid-air dogfight to gain those precious inches. And then Malibu was HIT... HIT...and *HIT* again, before he came down.

A hushed crowd awaited the referees' signal.

2nd and inches!

The crowd groaned.

The pile of Chinese robots peeled off Kingman. He was slow getting to his feet. Suddenly, he keeled to one side. Regaining his balance, panic seized him. He tried but couldn't make a fist with his right hand!

The doctor's warning echoed in his head. "You could wind up paralyzed for the rest of your life!"

109

Inside the secret lab filled with robot heads of the president, Newton waited for his hostage's reaction. "Well?"

"Everything is justified as a means to our more perfect union."

"I don't understand."

"Of course not. To leave the governing of society to capricious humans and their irrational and unpredictable natures is a thing of the past. Obsolete! Like you."

The lab's security system, identical to the one at NAFA, had been alerted that Newton's voiceprint matched that of the "intruder" who'd wreaked havoc earlier.

"Only the perfect logic of our robotic technologies," Newton declared, "can provide the enlightened rule necessary for the good of the world. A new age is dawning and I'm its—"

An alarm sounded. Newton's clearance had been revoked.

To his horror, a laser net targeted him. Before he could make his escape, he was imprisoned inside a white-hot laser cage! He tried shooting out the lasers, but couldn't hit them. As the sizzling light bars closed in on him, he implored the president.

"I can offer you the means to absolute rule. Not just of America but of the entire world! Together we can fulfill the Founding Father's dream for this country. There's an override mechanism. If you'll just follow my directions."

The president watched him dispassionately.

Newton pointed his laser at him. "Either we both get out of here alive, Mr. President, or no one does!"

The president seemed unfazed by Newton's threat.

The light cage grew smaller, closing in on Newton. He had only seconds....

"You fool!" he yelled. "What's wrong with you?! Do you want to die?!"

The president remained stoic and unmoved.

"Well, *die*!" Newton fired his laser at point-blank range.

The president's head exploded. It was a robot!

At first Newton was shocked, then crushed by the realization that it was Joy who had betrayed him.

The terrible hiss of seared flesh was drowned out by his blood-curdling screams.

110

"Humans! Humans! Humans!"

The roaring Ultra Bowl crowd was on its feet as the U.S. or rather the Humans were threatening to score with the clock running out.

China 44 – USA 38.

In the huddle, IQ noticed Kingman trying to flex his fist as he called the next play. A pass.

Kingman tried to hide his limp as he hobbled up to the line of scrimmage. He bobbled the snap and rolled to his right, his limp slowing him down, looking for IQ in the end zone. He barely got the ball away before he was smothered by the charging robot pass rush.

The pass was overthrown.

The crowd groaned.

3rd and inches.

Kingman had difficulty getting to his feet. His right leg buckled. He had trouble standing. Knights quickly surrounded and propped him up.

In the huddle, everyone sensed his distress. He could barely move his fingers!

With the doctor's warning echoing in his head, Kingman fought back his fear. He wasn't going to make the same mistake he made in the Super Bowl. "We got time for one more play."

"It's only 3rd down," Reggie protested.

Through gritted teeth, Kingman hissed, "This is it!" This was his last chance at redemption. "Screen to Malibu."

Everyone in the huddle was stunned.

"You crazy?!"

"You're the decoy!"

"No protection!"

"You're gonna be run over by a tank!"

IQ finally said what everyone was thinking. "It's *suicide!*"

Kingman laughed. "This whole damn game isn't too good for your health! But it'll be worth it if we score."

Malibu grabbed Kingman's facemask. "I'll die trying, Duke! I swear!"

As the U.S. lined up, Kingman had trouble standing behind Reggie to take the snap. He looked around at the hushed crowd in the stadium, then at China's terrifying robot "goal line" defense. It was so quiet he could almost hear the hum of their microprocessors. He tried flexing his hand—his fingers barely moved! He took a deep breath and barked out the numbers until the ball was snapped....

He couldn't feel the football and almost fumbled it, then stumbled as he dropped back.

Meanwhile, the Knights' offensive line held the fearsome robot pass rush for a count of five.

Malibu blocked an onrushing robot linebacker as it barreled for Kingman.

In unison, the offensive line released their blocks and let the robots through.

Kingman kept hobbling backwards, drawing the robot rush towards him.

Malibu disengaged from his block and looked back to Kingman for the short pass over the pass-rushing robots. He waved to get his attention, but Kingman was in trouble.

His leg kept buckling so he couldn't plant his foot to throw. And he couldn't grip the ball in his increasingly paralyzed hand.

Meanwhile, half a dozen robots—their throttles wide open—bore down on him.

Finally, he got his leg to hold and, with every last ounce of strength he possessed, willed his increasingly numb and paralyzed fingers to close around the football. He reared back and threw....

He didn't see what happened next because he was violently swept under by moving tidal wave of titanium robots—his body twisted every which way before he was finally buried under tons of metal!

And the pass? A wobbly, feeble one—not Kingman's usual tight spiral—that barely traveled the 15 yards to Malibu. And it was wide of the mark!

But the Artful Dodger, with a spectacular move, one-handed the ball, tucked it away and headed for the goal line.

At the 10-yard line, with the help of his jet-shoes, he turned on the after-burners. At the 4-yard line, he was about to leap into the air when he confronted a wall of Oriental demons making their goal line stand.

There was no way into the end zone but the hard way. So he bit down on his mouthpiece and began to slice, slash and spin—breaking tackles, bouncing off one robot after another, fighting for every inch! His rib broke! His knee shattered! But his legs kept churning! And finally, with a straight arm that fractured his elbow, he smashed his way across the goal line.

Touchdown!

China 44 - USA 44.

The pile of robots that buried Kingman peeled off, revealing the Knights' quarterback lying motionless on the ground.

Coach Merlin raced onto the field. He knelt over Kingman who opened his eyes and looked questioningly at his coach. Then he heard the crowd's thunderous chant.

"We did it!" Coach Merlin told him, fighting back tears. "*You* did it!

Kingman registered the news. With a sigh, he closed his eyes as a smile slowly spread across his face.

Triumphant Knights gathered around him. Their jubilation dampened by the sight of his motionless body. Lifting their quarterback carefully onto a stretcher, they carried him off the field as the hysterical crowd chanted, *"Humans! Humans! Humans!"*

Boom Boom kicked the extra point.

Pandemonium swept through Ultra Bowl stadium.

Up in their booth the announcers were hysterical. "They did it! My god, they did it! I can't believe it! Listen to *that*!! They did it! Oh my god!"

The crowd chanted, *"Humans! Humans!! Humans!!!"*

Carried away by the thunderous emotion sweeping the stadium, the announcers were delirious. "Incredible! They won! They *won*!! *We* won!!"

PART X

The Impossible

111

Malibu emerged from his hospital room. Though he leaned on crutches and wore two casts, he began hobbling down the hall.

IQ—his arm in a sling, a brace around his neck—with the aid of a cane limped out of his room. As Malibu walked by, IQ joined him.

One by one, convalescing Knights emerged from their hospital rooms and joined the "parade" of wounded warriors marching down the hall.

The parade halted outside Kingman's room.

Inside, Kingman sat in a wheelchair pushed by a nurse. Coach Merlin stood by his side.

"I'll take it from here," IQ told the nurse as he limped over to take her place behind Kingman's wheelchair.

"A promise is a promise," Malibu reminded Kingman. Despite the crutches, casts and bandages, he managed to offer his palm for a "low five."

Kingman just stared at it.

Malibu looked at him, then at Coach Merlin, then back at Kingman. "Oh Jesus! Oh no!"

112

Joy lay unconscious in a hospital bed while a doctor checked her vital signs.

An anxious Fig sat by her bedside. The doctor gave Fig a reassuring pat on the shoulder then left.

Out in the hall, the doctor was confronted by the Knights. "All I can tell you right now is that she's stable," he informed them. "But she's still unconscious. We've done everything we can. We'll just have to wait and see."

The news weighed heavily on the Knights, especially Kingman.

"Doctor! Doctor!!" Fig yelled from inside the room.

Propped up in bed, Joy's face lit up as Knights filled her room.

"You did it!" she exclaimed, tears in her eyes. Seeing Kingman, she reached out to him. "You did it!"

He didn't respond.

At first she was confused, but then she noticed his wheelchair, the long faces of his teammates and finally Kingman's gloomy expression.

"Nooo!!!" she cried out.

Kingman rocked back and forth, frantically trying to turn his wheelchair around. "Get me outa here!!"

IQ started to wheel him out, but Joy scrambled out of bed and threw herself in front of Kingman. Coach Merlin caught her and, with the doctor's help, carried her back to bed.

"She's still weak and needs to rest," the doctor said as he herded everyone out of the room.

One of the last to leave, Kingman stopped IQ. "Give me a minute."

Once he and Joy were alone, Kingman sat silently in his wheelchair unable to look at her.

"I'll be there for you," she finally said, breaking the tortured silence. "I'll be your arms and legs. I'll—"

"I don't want your damn pity!" he hissed.

"That won't be necessary," the doctor interjected as he walked back into the room.

Kingman shot him a withering look.

"What are you saying?" Joy asked him.

"From our preliminary tests, I'm confident we can regenerate the damaged nerve tissue."

Kingman was stunned. "But...but that's *impossible*!"

"Not at all, Mr. Kingman. We do nerve transplants all the time."

Kingman recalled the last thing his doctor had said on that dreaded day when he warned him not to play. "I'm sorry, Duke. Maybe someday we'll be able to do nerve transplants, but not for a good long while."

"Isn't that wonderful news?!" Joy exclaimed, startling Kingman out of his reverie.

"You have an excellent chance for a complete recovery," the doctor informed him.

"Thank you, doctor!" Joy said tearfully, as she took Kingman's paralyzed hand. "Thank you!"

113

In his hospital room, IQ tried to show Fig a card trick. But his cast and bandages got in the way. Frustrated, he handed Fig the deck. "*You* shuffle!"

Fig did.

IQ was impressed. "You're pretty good!"

Fig smiled. "I've been practicing."

Reggie popped his head through the door. "Hey, shake a leg! Got a plane to catch! Don't want to keep the president waiting."

When Reggie left, IQ fished something out of his bag. "Almost forgot this." He handed Fig one of the Knights' NFL footballs. "It's for you."

On his way out the door, he turned to Fig. "Want me to give the president any message?"

Fig didn't hear him; he was staring in awe at the "antique" football. "Would you sign it?"

Touched, IQ muttered, "Got a pen?"

114

Malibu and Coach Merlin huddled together with Kingman in a corner of Joy's room while Dr. Christianson paid her a visit.

"You're looking much better," she said, pleased to see him at her bedside.

"I've quit drinking."

They shared a long look.

"Thank you for trusting me," she said. "Was the decoy your idea?"

"You handed it to me," he replied with a knowing smile, referring to their encounter at the NAFA banquet. "I'm sorry about your uncle."

Despite herself, Joy eyes filled with tears. "He was... an *evil* man."

"Misguided," Christianson offered. "But brilliant."

"What happened to my father's....?"

"Gone."

She sighed.

"I'm sorry. Your uncle's secret labs were manned by bots he'd programmed to insure maximum security. Talk about black ops. This was a black hole. Only he and his bots knew about it. If it hadn't been for you, we'd never—"

"It was purely by accident..."

"Newton thought of everything. He programmed the entire lab and all the bots who worked there to self-destruct if his vital signs ever flatlined. The moment he died, it all went up in smoke. Metaphorically speaking."

"How do you know all this?" she asked.

"Well, this is the really strange part. All of Newton's bots self-destructed. Even his most trusted aide. All except one."

"Really?!" Joy's mind was ablaze with curiosity.

A smile slowly unfurled on Christianson's face. "His FemBot."

Joy's mouth dropped open.

"We were able to access her memory and unravel his entire plot."

Puzzled, Joy wondered, "Why? Why did he leave her?"

Christianson sighed. "Maybe he *loved* it."

Joy tried to comprehend this man whom she'd loved and hated, who'd given her so much and taken so much away, who was so brilliant and yet so evil. Finally, she shook her head.

"Love..." she repeated wistfully, "it makes you do crazy things."

"Time to go," Coach Merlin announced from across the room.

Joy offered Christianson her hand. "Congratulations on being named Director."

"Thanks. I hope you'll stay on. We have a lot of work to do at NAFA if we're going to fulfill your father's vision."

Coach Merlin wheeled Kingman over to Joy's bedside. Despite his crutches, Malibu kept up. "Man, I wish you were coming," he told Kingman.

"Just won't be the same without you," Coach Merlin echoed.

"Wish I was going, too," Kingman replied.

"They want to operate as soon as possible," Joy explained.

"Great!" Malibu said, "I hear they're gonna put you back together good as new!"

Christianson chimed in. "And if you're not completely satisfied, I can bionicize you and personally guarantee your satisfaction."

"Will you throw in the first 3,000 mile oil change for free?" Malibu cracked.

From Christianson's perplexed expression, it was clear he didn't get the joke.

The Knights, however, burst into laughter.

115

The team was flown on their "vintage" 21st century plane—piloted by the original crew who had been separately quarantined—to Washington, D.C. The Knights were going to be the guests of honor at a state dinner hosted by the President and First Lady. There was some speculation that they might even be awarded their country's highest honor—the Congressional Medal of Honor.

This was a very different plane ride than their previous one as Super Bowl losers. They were Ultra Bowl winners! So corks popped and champagne flowed as the plane filled with gales of laughter from their mid-air celebration.

"Now this is more like it!"

"Washington here we come!"

"You think there'll be ticker tape?"

"We're heroes! Honest-to-god heroes!"

"Dude, we gonna be wined and dined by the Prez himself!"

"God, I wish the fans back home could see us now!"

The Knights were partying so hard, it's doubtful anyone saw the strange yet familiar cloud they were heading towards.

116

Transfixed by the screen in her hospital room, Kingman, Joy and Fig were aghast as a grim president addressed the nation.

"It is with the greatest sadness that I inform you that the plane carrying our Ultra Bowl team, the heroic New York Knights, has disappeared. Our scientists have detected the same unusual space-time disturbances that preceded their appearance a week ago. Though the Chronos Protocol laboratory was destroyed, this may be what our scientists speculate is a 'rebound effect' or 'echo' from the original time-dilation experiment."

Joy looked at Kingman in his wheelchair.

Fig kept murmuring, "Holy Iaccoca!"

"For this reason," the president continued, "we believe their plane has flown through the same time warp from which they came...and that they've returned to their own time in the past."

Sensing Joy watching him, Kingman turned and saw the unasked question in her eyes.

"This is where I belong!" he answered. "Where I was meant to be!"

The president continued, "We owe these men so much. We owe them our profoundest gratitude for reminding us who we once were. And for showing us who we can still be."

Joy wanted more than anything to embrace Kingman. But she hesitated, unsure how he'd respond. And, of course, Fig was watching them.

Meanwhile, Kingman tried to get a handle on this shocking news. Terrible? Wonderful? Alternating waves of dizzying emotions coursed through him. Unable to move, he was defenseless. In desperation, he looked around for some distraction and noticed the football Fig held tightly against his chest. "What ya got there?"

Fig showed it to him. "They all signed it!" he announced proudly.

Seeing his teammates' signatures overwhelmed him. "They're the greatest bunch of guys in the world!" he muttered. Fighting for control, he continued, "I'm gonna add my name, Fig, I swear! Meanwhile, you hang onto it. We've got lots of work to do if we're gonna turn you into a quarterback!"

The president concluded his address to the nation. "On behalf of every American, I wish the Knights a safe journey home."

117

The Knights' plane landed at JFK and taxied to a specially designated runway. A stunned and disoriented team disembarked. On the tarmac, cordoned off by police, throngs of disappointed fans and a rabid media corps waited. Apparently no time had passed—it was the night of their Super Bowl loss.

Many in the crowd were surprised by the shaven heads sported by all the players. When questioned about it, TJ replied, "Penance for the sin of losing."

But more than their new haircuts, the crowd was taken aback by the extent of the Knights' injuries. Someone from ESPN called out, "You guys look like you've been through a war. From where I sat, the game didn't look that brutal."

"Nah," Reggie said straight-faced. "We just had a bumpy flight home!"

A sleazeball reporter stuck his mike in Hacksaw's face. "You guys think you wuz robbed?"

Hacksaw waxed philosophic—"Ya win some, ya lose some."

A New York Post reporter tried to interview IQ. "You just lost the Super Bowl, but you don't seem that upset. You act like you won. What's going on?"

IQ looked at the cameras and deadpanned. "We're just good losers. That's the mark of real champions, isn't it!"

Someone in the crowd yelled, "Where's Duke Kingman?" Others echoed him.

"On vacation," Malibu said, a big smile on his face.

"Coach, will Kingman be back next year?"

The sleazeball reporter piled on. "Where did Kingman go?"

Hacksaw picked the guy up by his shirt and held him in the air. "Where assholes like you can't bother him!"

A Chinese reporter with a thick accent stuck a mike in their faces. "Your injuries make one wonder if football is too violent, too dangerous, to be played by humans?"

This stopped the Knights dead in their tracks. They exchanged looks and couldn't help but wonder—did this incident provoke the Ultra Bowl in the first place?!

Coach Merlin ended the impromptu press conference. "Boys, it's great to be back! Just great! We gave it everything we had. We did our best. I've never been prouder of a team! And now we'd like to go home."

118

Joy tenderly kissed Kingman's hands. From his delighted reaction, it was obvious that the operation was a complete success. They embraced and began making love.

Through their bedroom window a much thinner and fitter Fig could be seen outside playing quarterback. He dropped back to pass...to his new dog...while simultaneously doing the play-by-play.

"Fig Newton drops back to pass... Holy IQ-coca is going deep, deep...."

He reared back and threw. It was a decent spiral but overthrown, sailing over the dog's head and crashing into the bedroom window, startling the two lovers.

Looking out their shattered window, Kingman and Joy saw Fig petting his dog. Fig looked up in their direction, shrugged sheepishly and waved.

The lovers looked at each and burst out laughing.

STAY CONNECTED

If you'd like to receive updates about the latest developments in the Ultra Bowl saga (there's a movie & video game in the works), as well as alerts about forthcoming adventures in the "*Chronos Protocol*" series, write UltraBowlBook@gmail.com and we'll keep you informed.

UltraBowlBook@gmail.com

www.UltraBowlBook.com

www.IJWeinstock.com

About the Author

I. J. Weinstock has enjoyed a varied career in the arts as an actor, artist and award-winning author. Besides the sci-fi novel *ULTRA BOWL*, his recent books include: *JOYride: How My Late Wife Loved Me Back To Life*, which won an eLit Award—silver medal for *Best Inspirational/ Spiritual Digital Book* of 2011; *Grief Quest: A Workbook & Journal to Heal the Grieving Heart*, named a FINALIST in the 2012 USA Best Book Awards; and *The LoveSpell Secret: A 30-Day Heaven-Sent Program to Create More Love in Your Life.*

His latest novel, *The Secret Sex Life of Angels*, is the first in a series about the magic & mystery of sex. One hundred days into his presidency, Adam Hart discovers that to fulfill his oath of office he must embark on a secret sexual odyssey that could determine the fate of the world.

You'll Never Look At Sex In The Same Way Again!

www.IJWeinstock.com

I. J. Weinstock played football in high school and describes how it influenced his life.

It was on a football field that I learned an important life lesson. During the summer of my sophomore year in high school,

I came down with mono. In the fall, I tried out and made the varsity football team. At the time, I didn't know it would be months before I fully recovered. Though I attended school, I wasn't feeling well enough to play. After a couple of weeks I had to quit the team.

Quitting was unacceptable to the coaches. The next summer, fully recovered, I trained every day in a park in preparation for football tryouts. I vowed I'd be in the starting lineup on opening day. I'll never forget the day a coach saw me and asked what I was doing. "Getting ready for football season," I told him. His response—"You're wasting your time."

I showed up for tryouts, but was shunned. Though a senior, I was given freshman uniforms and ostracized in every possible way. No matter how hard I worked, I was ignored and, at most, assigned to carry equipment for the team.

After several weeks of being invisible on the field (not being picked for teams or drills) and being abused like Richard Gere in the movie "An Officer and a Gentleman," my quest seemed an exercise in futility. I was ready to quit. Again.

Dejected, I was sitting alone in the locker room after practice when one of the coaches came over and whispered, "Keep it up." I did and began to be picked for drills. I was on fire! On opening day I started on the first string varsity football team as a wide receiver and defensive cornerback.

To cap off my high school comeback fairy tale, on a crisp Saturday afternoon in October, I won the Homecoming Day game with a 63-yard touchdown. When the town newspaper ran a front-page story with my picture, I began to think I could do anything I set my heart on.

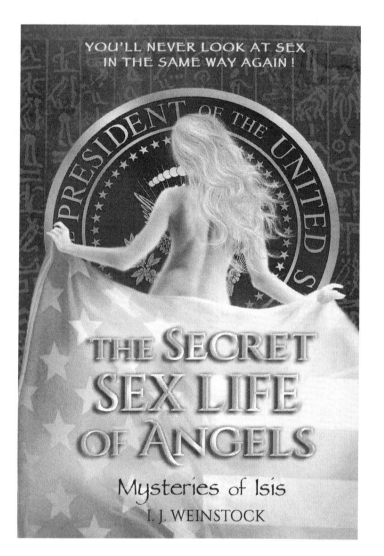

YOU'LL NEVER LOOK AT SEX
IN THE SAME WAY AGAIN !

THE SECRET
SEX LIFE
OF ANGELS

Mysteries of Isis

I. J. WEINSTOCK

The Ultimate Secret

In a world with no future, one man is offered a secret key from the past to unlock the greatest mystery of all.

One hundred days into his presidency, Adam Hart discovers that to fulfill his oath of office he must embark on a sexual odyssey that could determine the fate of the world.

The Secret Sex Life of Angels combines the intrigue and controversy of *The Da Vinci Code* with the spirituality and eroticism of the *Kama Sutra* in a fantastic saga about the sacred nature of sex.

"Every man needs to read *The Secret Sex Life of Angels*.
Every woman needs to have her man read this book."

"You'll never think about sex in the same way again!"

"This is the book everyone will be talking about."

**Find out more about *The Secret Sex Life Angels*
visit www.IJWeinstock.com**

43530680R00183

Made in the USA
San Bernardino, CA
21 December 2016